Indigo After Dark

Genesis Press's new imprint goes beyond sensuous. It's romantic erotica that is tasteful, classy and vividly sexual—in short, it's hot but not pornographic. Here's what some of the readers had to say about Indigo After Dark.

The stories give just the amount of tease to entice the reader to breathe hard and wish to be inside the pages of the book. Thank you, Tracye.

I'm in my twelfth year of marriage, and reading these stories gives me plenty of ideas and helps me to recreate the romance that has dwindled away.

MORE, MORE, MORE! This is exactly what I've been waiting for—AA romance. Bravo Genesis!.

This is great!! It's erotic without being vulgar. I can't wait until this line is on the book shelves.

Romantic, yes, but even more so, in a sexy romantic type of fantasy. These stories seem to be geared toward a more mature female reader, like myself.

I think this is just what we need, some seduction along with some romance. I'll definitely buy this book.

The sexual overtures were a turn on. It's nice to know that passion exists between two people. Can't wait for the book to come out.

So go on, what are you waiting for? Your fantasies await you on the other side of this page. Indulge.

Indigo After Dark

is published by

Genesis Press, Inc.
315 Third Avenue North
Columbus, MS 39701

Indigo After Dark, Vol. II
Brown Sugar Diaries & The Forbidden Art of Desire

First Edition

Indigo After Dark

Vol. II

Romantic Erotica...for women

Genesis Press, Inc.

Caution:

Reading this book causes extreme stimulation, lust and exquisite languor.

Brought to you by

Indigo After Dark

an Imprint of

Genesis Press, Inc.

Indigo After Dark...

Beyond Sensuous

Vol. II

Brown Sugar Diaries

by

Dolores Bundy

The Forbidden Art of Desire

by

Cole Riley

Table of Content

Brown Sugar Diaries by Dolores Bundy
PART I

The Forbidden Art of Desire by Cole Riley
PART II

Brown Sugar Diaries

by
Dolores Bundy

About Ena

It was almost dawn when Ena lit her first cigarette, taking long, deep draws before crushing it out. When she was fully awake, she pulled herself away from her cozy down-feathered bed and lazily sauntered over to the three tall bay windows lining her huge L-shaped bedroom, threw open the shutters, then the windows. It was nearly spring in Manhattan, and tiny delicate flowers hung gingerly from rows of honeysuckle trees and filled the air with a redolent smell of sweetness. The crisp morning air was exhilarating as she let it slowly revive her, breathing deeply, embracing the fresh morning dew with arms stretched wide. Majestically unfolding before her was the certainty of dawn's magnificence, illuminating her body to a creamy bronzed perfection against the beauty of the morning's sunlight. She pondered when she had last seen such beauty and felt so good. Her last visit to Belgium, when looking out onto the square from the Carrefour De L'Europe in Brussels, was surely another glorious moment like this one, she thought.

In thinking about her travels abroad, she promised herself she would take more time with her friends on the next trip. She would visit Heather and Stuart in London and Donny in Amsterdam, maybe even Xavier in Stuttgart and her friends Jimmy and Bettina who lived in Bonn, Germany.

Ena stood nude before the window as she did most mornings, looking out at the Hudson River in deep reflection. Riverside Drive had not changed all that much through the years, she thought. Its characteristics of quaint buildings and cobblestone streets were structured many years ago and gloriously maintained. Ena thought fondly of her friends living on their boats anchored at the Seventy-ninth Street boat basin, who enjoyed the perfectly timed seasonal changes surrounding the trees and river as she did. She envisioned rows of harbor lights skating across the silk-clad river clearly to New Jersey. She realized how much she really missed this magnificent place whenever she traveled.

Ena was comfortable in at least a dozen cities around the world but when thinking of them collectively, none gave her the continual thrust and vitality of New York City. She loved the Naked City, and it seemed to endear itself to her. At thirty-two, she was more beautiful than ever. She was a striking woman, an exotic creature who stood taller than most women. Her provocative ways, often exhibited by a bewitching magic of expression, clearly caught people's imagination. She possessed an empowering life force of charisma that was puzzling to some, uncanny to others, but to those who knew her, it was mostly a gift. Deeply rooted in her character was an insatiable lust for life. She loved power players, dynasty dreamers and men much too young for her.

Ena swayed over to the white, gold-framed dressing table standing opposite her canopy bed and scanned her appointment book. Penciled in was a morning meeting with her modeling agency, a go-see appointment at noon and a meeting with her lawyer later that evening.

Ena returned from overseas, tired, bored and weary. She had become the target of criticism recently for having posed for the British men's magazine *Arena*. Shown totally undressed in a twenty-five-page photo essay, her poses had provoked furor—controversial pictures that some people called depraved. In one picture, she was shown lying on a kitchen table with her right leg raised, holding a rolling pin in her left hand, touching herself. On the table there was an empty egg carton, a pan with flour and a just-baked phallic-shaped cookie. In another photo, she held a big black nightstick, wearing just a police cap, bra and no panties. On the cover, she appeared nude, riding bareback on a white Arabian horse with a diamond tiara placed on her head.

Ena gazed in the trifold mirror, contemplating her own slightly frazzled image, when the young man she brought home the previous night began to stir. The barely twenty-five-year-old, passively raised his head above the pillow, and wiped the sleep from his deep, sullen eyes. He raked his finely knit curly hair, smoothing it down along his neck. She watched him as the red silk sheets sloped down his bronze muscular physique, exposing broad shoulders and thick fully haired chest. With eyes glued

2

to his body, she fixed on his well-formed hardness as he looked at her through piercing jade eyes and smiled.

"Good morning, Ena," he whispered, and beckoned her with a kiss.

She was smiling sweetly when she went to him; her body warm and responsive. She slipped into bed close to him and slid down his hard body, feeling his sex along the inside of her thighs. His rippling stomach muscles pressed against her full, tender breasts, and the slenderness of her body intertwined with his like a cunning snake. She cupped her breasts and cooed and gyrated when he entered her. Together, they soared into a whirlwind of passion.

He glided up and down her walls with a smooth, soothing motion. Her juices flowed lovingly as he turned her body on its side, lifted her legs and opened them wide. He slid himself deep inside her with an unwavering movement that penetrated her feminine hearth, and a torrent heat rushed to her head. His tantalizing pulsation hurled her emotions into an uncontrollable state of lust, and seconds later, revealed she was weeping. Her resign was the passage he needed to claim his conviction. With increased purpose, he propelled himself deeper. A reeling outpour, plodded, plowed and plunged. Ena was near explosion when she screamed out. "Ooooh! Please...stop!" And pushed him away.

"What's wrong?" he questioned. "What did I...Did I..."

Ena quieted him with a low, sultry voice. "Shhh...Don't talk." Her voice was trembling. "Just go!"

A cool breeze brushed over them as Ena suddenly tossed the sheets away from her quivering body and jumped out of bed. He attempted to kiss the soft curvature of her shoulder but she shrugged him off.

"What's wrong, Ena...What did I do?"

He watched Ena float across the floor and bend from the waist to place kindling in the fireplace. Her round bottom and fully haired privata stared him right in the face. He desperately wanted her, right then and there with no resistance, but when she looked back at him, her face was expressionless...

"You're...torturing me, Ena," he cried. "What's happening with you? "What's wrong?" he asked, confused. Ena saw his perplexity but ignored it and yawned as she watched the fire begin to blaze. The vibrancy of the colors provoked images of their lovemaking, adding an

3

element of warmth against her nakedness. She would miss him terribly, she thought, but their passionate lovemaking was only a momentary thirst quencher, an insatiable lust, quieted. The young Adonis was saddened by the surrender. He zipped up his pants and pulled on his sweater.

If passion had a taste, he thought, it would be the taste of Ena.

"Ena, won't you tell me what's wrong?"

"I'll call you...I promise," she responded and yawned again, making animal sounds and taking long, deep breaths, absorbing the distinctly nutty aroma coming from the fire.

"I'll call you!" she repeated. "I promise."

The young man threw on his jacket, gestured as if to salute her and walked to the door. He looked back, hoping for one last glimpse of the woman he had never gotten to know, didn't understand and beyond that would probably never see again, but she was not there.

He stepped out into the fresh morning air, harboring feelings of resentment and forlorn. He thought of something a friend once told him about women like Ena. A beautiful woman is yours, he told him, only if she comes back to you after she has experienced all the world has to offer, or forsakes all things for you from the beginning! His friend must be right, he thought as he stepped into the nearly spring air, saddened, accompanied by his friend's words.

Ena watched the glint of light shine brilliantly on the ebbing river's edge when the doorbell rang. It was Fernanda, a dear friend who recently posed for a Calvin Klein's jeans campaign with her overseas and became well-known instantly for her rare Latino beauty. The dark-eyed bronzed knockout wore sunglasses. Her eyes were swollen with tears, and a fearful look covered her face.

"What's happened to you, Fern," Ena asked as she opened the door.

Fernanda fainted. Falling to the floor, her coat fell open, and Ena could see she was completely nude. Faded bruises covered her frail body. Ena lifted her onto the sofa and ran into the bedroom, returning with blankets. She covered Fernanda and embraced her.

"Oh, Fern. What's happened to you!"

"Ena, I just want to die," she cried.

"Who did this? Paulo?"

"No, not Paulo. Paulo's father."

"His father!" Ena shouted. "Are you kidding me?"

"We made love...and...I guess it got out of hand."

Ena touched Fernanda's body lovingly, smoothing her hand over the bruises and caressed her.

"I'm sorry, Fern. You didn't deserve this," she assured her and kissed her neck.

"Stay here with me. Together we'll figure out what to do."

Ena and Fernanda could not forget how they got their work in this city. The Majouirn Agency was run by Paulo, but his father Carlo owned it. Making love to Carlo was part of the scheme of things; all the models got their start that way.

Ena picked up the phone and called Carlo. She urged him to meet her at her penthouse for their appointment, and he agreed. Ena and Fernanda smiled at each other and waited patiently for him.

The dumpy five-foot-six man smiled slyly when Ena opened the door. He was punctual, just as always. Ena offered him a seat and excused herself. When she returned, she approached him from behind and wrapped a tie around his neck. Fernanda walked around in front of him and opened her coat. She was nude, and her bruises were obvious. The man's mouth flew open as the two gagged him. They stripped him naked then tied his hands and feet. Fernanda fondled his short, stumpy penis and laughed loudly.

"This little piggy went to market," she taunted, wriggling his little wiggly penis.

Ena joined in the teasing, laughing. "This little piggy stayed home! And this little piggy went wee wee wee...all the way home!"

Ena and Fernanda yanked and pulled his penis and pinched him. To his horror, they turned him over and began popping his bottom until red prints were all over him. Fernanda ran in the kitchen and pulled out several ice trays and threw ice cubes on him while Ena rubbed them all over his body.

He screamed in terror...

"I didn't mean to hurt you, Fernanda. I don't know what came over me!"

"Oh! You know, you greedy prick," she said.

5

"You'll make it up to her, won't you?" Ena hollered.

"Say you're sorry, creep, and we want more overseas work...right?"

"Whatever you want. Just stop, please!"

The two women began making love in front of him, torturing his ego...

"See this," Fernanda said, opening her legs and jamming her pussy in his face.

"Smell it! she jolted. "And smell it good. This is as far as you'll ever get to this pretty pussy again. Ena stripped her panties and fondled Fernanda's breasts. Fernanda pulled out a dildo and shoved it in her. Together they moaned and groaned. The man was humiliated when they bent over him and patted each other's clit and suckled each other then rubbed their clits together.

"Now, hear me and hear me good," Ena demanded. "I'll cut your wiggle off the next time you pull this stupid shit again or you approach either of us."

The women fondled each other and continued to taunt him.

Fernanda opened the window and threw out his clothing. Ena untied him and shoved him out of the door and slammed it behind him, laughing crazily.

She screamed out of the window... "There's a robber outside our door, please come quickly!"

Ena and Fernanda laughed and giggled together as they planned whom they might pick up that evening and lay, and their next visit overseas, first-class accommodations, of course.

To Zoe, with Love

She strummed her guitar, dreaming through a bottle of brandy. She dreamed of sugar cane, snowcapped mountains and pure champagne and men who smelled like air...

"*Curitiba! Curitiba! Curitiba!*" she sang. *Curitiba—me home ... Brazil!*"

Her dark-rimmed eyes flashed to the rhythm of a child's heartbeat and the mystic of the samba that rolled inside her...

"*Curitiba! Curitiba! Curitiba!*" she sang. "*Curitiba—me home... Brazil! Me lambuzza de cana, tabaco e rum...Curitiba—me home... Brazil!*"

She posed with provoked furor, clutched her guitar and swayed her hips to the African rhythms that gripped her body...

"I make love to the wind!" she cried.

"*Nosa musica tem sangue tropical...Curitiba—me home...Brazil!*"

The music swelled, wrapping her body with popping guitars, wailing trumpets and the roar of the bouncing crowd. She bolstered a leg high above her head and shoved the guitar between her stance. Her hypnotic eyes widened with the beam of the spotlight as she danced and skipped and plucked and strummed...

"*Teu par anda? o Brazil!*" she shouted. "*Curitiba—me home... Brazil!*"

She threw the guitar in a heated passion and flung her arms in the air. She bracketed her hips with both hands, kicked back her heels and rocked from side to side...

"*Teu par anda? o Brazil!*" she called. "*Curitiba—me home...Brazil!*"

Suspended from her bouncing bare breasts and from her hips and thighs sparkled shimmering sequences of color. Glittering sapphires and dark emerald trinkets dangled from the ringlets of her long, black hair.

The sweet sound of flutes began to flutter...

"Ooooh...oooooh...ooooh!" she moaned. "Ah...ah...ahhhhh!"

Overwhelmed by the rush, she dashed across the stage, picked up her guitar and wailed and sang in scatted riffs... *"Bah...dop! Bah...dop! Bah...dop! Wah...wah...wah! Mmm...badop... badop...badop! Mmm...wa...wa...wa..."*

She laughed at the surge and tossed trinkets to the crowd, one by one. Her intoxicating blue eyes widened against her darker skinned, mulatto beauty that mystified and taunted her audience. The crowd clamored as she rocked and flaunted her voluptuous bottom and removed her panties. She threw them to the crowd and smiled mysteriously from lips that shimmered the color of crimson, and patted between her legs.

"I have no past!" she cried. "My future uncertain...and my biggest fear is near. My man is gone...Nowhere to be found...And my life is all but forgotten. *Curitiba! Curitiba! Curitiba!*" she sang. *"Curitiba me—home...Brazil!"*

United by the passion and rhythms that bound them, Sandman slammed his drums with triple syncopated beats and shouted, *"Curitiba! Curitiba! Curitiba! Curitiba—me home...Brazil!"*

She wrung her body in circles, engaged by the whistling crowd. The stage darkened a lush olive color, and she appeared completely nude. Covered by a sheer veil, and her body intertwined with a snake, she draped its thickness over her and rocked and swayed. She quivered as the serpent slid over her exposed, hardened nipples, along her thighs and crept between her legs. She gyrated and swaggered with the sleek, cold moistness of the serpent's skin, flush against her heated body and began to tremble.

The riveting sound of steel drums intensified, and the crowd's roars swelled...

"*O que é isto? O que é isto? O que é isto?* they screamed. What is this? *Sim...sim...sim!* Yes...yes...yes! Bravo...bravo...bravo!" they shouted with both thumbs raised in the air.

"*Obrigado...obrigado!*" she called out, bowed and sashayed off the stage. The curtain slowly lowered with the sound of drowning percussions and the swell of claps and cheers...

8

It was the rainy season in Brazil, and the natives claimed that with every ounce of rainwater that flowed to the mouth of the mighty Amazon could feasibly supply New York City with water for sixty years. Zoe felt the season's claim in her bones. Her body ached with a deep dampness that brought on feelings of anxiety. She huddled close to Sandman, looking out at the rain as the taxi driver tracked speedily across town, offering little conversation. They lived in the modern capital of the southern state of Paraná, a place called Curitiba.

Although Curitiba was considered the first pedestrian-only city in Brazil and a center for environmental education, it seemed to have lost its vision. The city never had much to say for itself, chiefly populated by European immigrants. It had not enjoyed the benefit of native and African fonts that enriched popular culture in other regions. The cultural poverty and repression of leisure and creativity was blamed on the immigrants' puritan work ethic and excessive civic penny-pinching. From a Freudian point of view, Curitiba was an anal retention. The sin was avarice—to create was a waste and one creates only by excess. The theory that culture is produced only in response to great privation and the absence of popular humus was a consideration. But by exuberance, the great existential adventure of the middle class in Curitiba was essentially the lack of a creative counterpart to the consumption, a fact ascribed to prosperity.

Zoe and Sandman entered their torn-down flat, equipped with sofa, table and two chairs and a tiny bedroom and kitchen. Partly dirt and cobblestone streets were lined with shacks to the north and more shacks that cluttered the hillside to the south. Called a *favelas*—a slum area, probably overtaken by the lost vision—some houses were built on wooden stilts, protecting them from seasonal floodwater. But when it rained heavily, houses were completely washed away.

Strewn around the little place was an array of colorful costumes, boxes of jewelry and buckets of body paint lining the floor and along windowsills. Empty bottles of rum, brandy and ale filled the garbage pails, and musical instruments were cluttered in every corner.

Sandman and Zoe undressed methodically, lazily dropping their clothing at the front door. Zoe flipped on the radio, and they both jumped in the shower as they did most nights. They let the warm water

9

flush away the night's work, talked about painful memories, failed undertakings and plans for the future and held each other tightly. They were still in their twenties and considered by their parents to be failures. They struggled and scrimped from week to week, living up to their aesthetic dreams. They had cherished each other since childhood, studied classical piano for five years in their teens and played together with local groups in Curitiba. Abandoning piano early on to create what they called the real music in their hearts and soul, they were the new music makers of samba, funk, jazz, chanson, frevo and rock. They attributed their creative ability to their African heritage, although they were part European. They were most proud of their African roots. It was romantic to be descendants of slaves, they thought and placed high value on the warmth and spontaneity they shared. Their creativity was the highest form of energy they knew.

Zoe opened her legs for Sandman to soap her there. She loved the feeling of suds between her legs and his hands massaging her. Calming music played in the background as they were swept into each other's arms. They clung together, soaping their bodies. He soaped her nipples and massaged her breasts and between her legs. She soaped the length of his shaft, hardened with the gentleness of her touch. He slipped himself between her thighs and stroked gently, cupped her breasts and kissed her mouth...

"To Zoe, with love..." he whispered.

He ran his fingers across his guitar, standing upright by the shower. She watched his long, slim body reach over her and pick up the guitar and strum the strings lightly. She danced in tiny circles, wriggling her hips to the enchanting echoes of the guitar and the sweet, throaty sounds he made. She was a goddess, he thought, carved by the gods as he watched water run through her hair and smooth the ringlets. He draped the guitar over his shoulder, lifted her arms over her head and kissed her neck, breasts and between her thighs...

"To Zoe, with love..." he whispered and methodically ran the back of his fingers over the guitar strings and rocked himself back and forth between her legs...

"Na casa do ovo meu avo me viu me transformar." he sang. *"Em sexy Zoe, uma serpente magnetic...Sexy Zoe, perigosa como um reptil!"*

10

His rhythm moved her with a pureness of passion, and the torrid fire that flickered beneath her groin seared her heart.

"Uma jiboia, jararaca, cobra cascavel," he sang. *"Uma bandida, uma vampira, uma vila criel. Sexy Zoe, perigosa como um reptil."*

He groped her hips and slung himself between them.

"Perigosa, venenosa, magnetic...Envolvente, cintilante, etcetera," he shouted. *"Sexy Zoe, perigosa como um reptil..."*

He bowed his head and groped her clit with his tongue and sweetly sucked. She laid on the floor of the shower and opened her legs. Warm water trickled over her body and began to bead around her soaped pubic hairs. He swiped away the soap and stroked her with his fingers, lovingly reaching deep inside. She was trembling when he spread her legs wider, draped the width of the tub and cuddled her thighs around his head. He slurped and licked her length and fondly grabbed her hair, smoothing it away from her shoulders. He pulled her forward, and she nestled his head in her arms. Her body rippled and waved with his insertion as she faced her passion. Creamy, delicious sliding began to explore her deepest feelings as she raked her fingers through his hair and pulled him to her breasts. He licked her lovingly and nibbled and sucked. They were the same person, united by a resounding passion that resonated near their souls, ignited by the passion they shared. He stood her up against the wall of the shower and wrapped her legs around his body. A surge rolled inside him as he moved himself in and out and back and forth between her legs. A thunderbolt surged inside him as he passionately pulled her arms above her head. She screamed with lust when he shoved himself inside her, jerking and flaunting her felineness and surrounding her with spastic jolts of passion.

"To Zoe, with love..." he whispered. "To Zoe, with love!"

They shivered as warm water turned cooler, locked in each other's arms.

They met Marianna at noon at the Café Bohemia. It was a vegetarian restaurant by day and wild showplace Friday, Saturday and Sunday nights. Marianna, at twenty-three, was Brazil's premiere exotic dancer. With freckles and a not-very-appealing nose, she resembled Barbra Streisand. Her body was an art form in motion, a paean to her birth. Marianna, like Zoe and Sandman, was of mixed blood—European and African. They claimed they were similar in other ways, too. They thought urbane, like kings and queens but performed like commoners, raw and realistic.

They ordered *aracajes,* bean dumpling, and coconut milk pâté, and Zoe added *caraje,* a strong coffee...

"*Como vai,* Marianna?" Zoe began. "How are you, my love?"

"*Mais ou menos...*" Marianna replied. "So so...And you? *Como vai?*"

"*Boa,*" Zoe answered. "I'm good!"

"*Bom,*" Sandman said. "I'm good...good! Thanks for asking."

Zoe wasted no time coming to the point..."We play The Garota de Ipanema, next week. It's a special night for us. Some American promoters will be there, on tour with Hiroshima. It's a good place. Marianna, we want to add you to our show."

"*Sim, sim,* Zoe!" Marianna responded without forethought. "Oh, yes, yes...I am ready!"

It was no secret, Zoe and Sandman had caused quite a stir in Brazil, a near cult in entertainment...

"When do we hit?" Marianna asked.

"Nine sharp, next Friday night," Zoe answered and looked at Sandman.

Sandman nodded. "*Sim...*Nine o'clock! We will rehearse this week. Is that okay?"

"*Sim,*" Marianna agreed, and the three began to plan.

Nightlife in Leblon and Ipanema's markets were trendy clubs with excellent jazz. There were varied choices for them to play. Botafogo, was one area. It had popular clubs with dancing and samba and *Cinelândia.* Lapa in the center, had a lot of samba and *pagode.* Rio was less organized and more spontaneous and much of the nightlife happened on the streets in front of bars, restaurants and anywhere outside with room to drink and sing.

Ipanema was their choice, a mixed bag, with some good local hangouts and a strong tourist influence and a lot of sex for sale, which always attracted customers.

The Garota de Ipanema was lively, open-air dining and there were a few foreigners checking out the place. It was where Tom Jobim and

Vinicius de Moraes were sitting when they wrote "The Girl from Ipanema." A recent *Brazilian Playboy* survey rated its chops, the best. The restaurant boasted of having the finest shows and the most delicious *petiscos* food in Brazil.

The curtain raised slowly with the brilliant sounds of howler monkeys, barking and hooting raucous and squawking red, blue and green parrots. Toucans with banana-sized beaks and scarlet macaws spiraled overhead. A three-toed sloth hung upside down from hook like claws to the left of the stage. Four guitars strummed softly as Zoe descended, bolstered from the ceiling in an open cage. She was nude, and zebra stripes were painted over her entire body. From head to toe, colors of the rainbow spotlighted her entrance. She grasped the bars and gyrated.

A loud bang from clasping cymbals and a strong rhythmic drumbeat, vaulted the room. Caracas and loud clicks from wooden sticks accentuated the rhythm. A circular moving platform pulled Sandman center stage. He was seated behind a huge set of drums as he flung and twirled his drumsticks in the air. He rolled out with loud African-flavored drumbeats, smiling and playing like a madman.

Marianna appeared in a puff of translucent purple smoke. Her body was painted a brilliant bronze, and her hair, wildly arranged all over her head, laminated a bright white. The crowd stood as Marianna opened Zoe's cage door and entered. Their bodies meshed, merged in a caress as they licked each other's nipples, ringed in white circles and sharply pointed. They touched each other provocatively, rubbing their breasts together and kissed each other's thighs and between their legs. Marianna kissed Zoe's feet as if in tribute to the African god Zangu and twirled in circles. Spirited by Candomblé, the religion they practiced, brought to Brazil by their slave ancestors, Marianna whispered in Zoe's ear in Euroba language. They smiled at each other, united by the spirit they shared and twirled around and around, rubbing bottoms. They fell into each other's arms and slid to the floor intertwined in animated movements and crawled out of the cage. The stage lit up a splendid brilliance, a colorful assortment of flashing lights.

The mood changed, graced by the soothing sounds of violins and softly strummed guitars. The audience was awestruck when the spotlight began flashing, and Zoe and Marianna lifted each other's legs and rubbed their faces between. They wriggled along the floor, rubbing and sucking as the band broke into a wild samba rhythm. Marianna jumped up, kicked back her heels, swiveled her hips and laid on top of Zoe, gyrating over her body in loops and suspensions. She suddenly threw up Zoe's legs, slapped her bottom and adamantly began licking and sucking.

Zoe rolled over on top of Marianna, pinning her arms above her head. She sucked her pointed nipples, swiped her pubic mound and licked her fingers. She looked at the crowd as she stood over Marianna and swayed to the squealing trumpets that accentuated her body movements, grabbing, caressing and gyrating. She lifted Marianna, positioning her on all fours and mounted her.

Zoe grabbed the microphone and began to sing...
Pulso por dentro do pulso
Ritmo íntimo em mim
Mundo no fundo do fundo
Vida na vida sem fim...
Marianna bowed her head as Zoe pulled her hair and belted out...
Pulse inside a pulse
Intimate rhythm in me
World at the depth of the depth
Life in a life without end!
The crowd stood clapping as Zoe threw the microphone to the floor and spanked Marianna's bottom, inspired by an excitement that started Marianna bucking wildly. Zoe pushed back and forth on Marianna's wiggling body and felt Zoe's moistness against her back. Zoe stood erect as Marianna turned her body and lay flat on the floor. Marianna reached her tongue for Zoe, and Zoe squatted. Marianna began licking Zoe between her legs. Zoe spread her legs wider, dropping slowly into a split on Marianna's face. Marianna licked her opening and began fingering her as they rolled over on the floor. Marianna spread her legs as Zoe scooped up a mound of pubic hair, cupping it with both hands and began slurping. Marianna's back arched with a striate orgasm as Zoe sucked and slurped...

"Oooh...oooh...ooooh!" the crowd gasped, covering their mouths.

Zoe cupped Marianna's breasts, and the crowd pounded its feet. The sounds of howling monkeys and drumbeats came alive and encompassed the room. Zoe stroked Marianna's long, white hair, jerked her head back and kissed her fiery painted lips. They sucked each other and hugged and caressed, rubbing their pubic mounds together, grinding and churning their bodies.

A pole slowly extended from the ceiling and bolted onto the stage floor. Marianna began to climb, and Zoe followed, biting at her bottom like an animal. Marianna's opening undulated with every bite. Zoe sucked and fingered her moistness, smiled at the audience and licked her fingers and lips. Colorful spotlights flashed in every direction. Sounds of gut-wrenching guitars and violent drumbeats surged and flooded the room. Zoe sucked Marianna's bottom as they hung suspended from the pole being hoisted up toward the ceiling.

The promoters joined the group at Zeppelin Bar, behind the Sheraton Hotel on Avenida Niemeyer, a quaint bar and restaurant overlooking the ocean. It was medium-priced with great live folk and pop music and a very relaxed atmosphere. Zoe, Sandman and Marianna were pleased by the promoters' choice. They were very tired from the night's performance and wanted things to go well, but they wanted them to be brief so they could go home and relax. They ordered *Pichasa*, and the Americans ordered strong rum and sodas.

"How are you!" John began.

"Yeah, how are you, folks!" David echoed.

"Okay...okay!" Sandman responded, and Zoe and Marianna nodded their heads like children.

"We're glad you could come," John continued. "We realize you must be exhausted. I'll get right to the point...

"Our favorite bar is Bar Lagoa, Rio's oldest. It's in a town that's losing its traditions rapidly to modern Western schlock, but has changed little. Last year, neighborhood associations tried to close it down to build a high-rise, high-tech condo complex, but opposition was too strong. It's open to the public, seven-thirty in the evening until three in the morning...with food, drink and a loud Carioca crowd.

"We want your show for the after-hours party showcase. In the back is a private club and only the richest of the rich are members."

John and David looked at Sandman, and Sandman looked at Zoe. They knew the place and loved it. Zoe looked deeply into Marianna's eyes, felt her excitement and nodded.

"*Sim...sim!* You got a deal," Sandman said.

Zoe and Marianna smiled and kissed each other, then hugged Sandman.

John liked the show the way it was. David wanted to make some changes.

"...Add a little more flavor," he said. "More costumes...maybe add some American stuff to the repertoire...And in January and February, we do Rio, Carnival time!

"Then to the states...We're looking at working the states—Las Vegas, maybe first... some hot spots in Vegas."

"We're ready!" Sandman said and shook the men's hands. The men kissed Zoe and Marianna, and David summoned the driver.

"Take them where they want to go," John told the driver. "We'll be in touch! We'll discuss money, then."

"Yeah, money. We'll discuss money," David dittoed.

"Take us to Curitiba," Sandman instructed, and the driver took off.

Zoe and Marianna were excited, and Sandman loved them for it. They all stripped naked and lay on the floor, drinking Pichasa and dreaming up new ideas for future shows. Sandman extended his dick to Marianna, and she took him in her mouth, sucking his length slowly. Zoe licked Marianna's nipples and reached deep inside her with her fingers.

Sandman reached over Marianna, and took a sip of Pichasa and laid back on the sofa. His pulsation was on fire, festering with lust when he shoved into Zoe's pussy, vigorously pushing and pulling. Marianna began rubbing Zoe's clit and gripping her tits as Sandman shoved and jerked. Zoe's pussy immediately ignited an explosion that shot him out like a thunderbolt.

Sandman lay comfortably on the floor, grabbed Zoe's guitar and began to play. Marianna and Zoe continued to fondle each other, stuck on play.

"To Zoe, with love..." Sandman whispered and looked at Zoe and smiled. *"Na casa do ovo meu avo me viu me transforma,"* he sang and strummed. *"Em sexy Zoe, uma serpente magnetic. Sexy Zoe, perigosa como um reptil.* To Zoe, with love..."

"To Zoe, with love," Marianna whispered and bowed her head between Zoe's legs as Zoe lay quietly, strumming her guitar and cuddled in Sandman's arms. Marianna licked her moistness, and Sandman held her close...

She strummed her guitar, dreaming through a bottle of brandy. She dreamed of sugar cane, snowcapped mountains and pure champagne and men who smelled like air...

This is your tribunal, the wind cried. It must be true, she replied, and rocked herself to sleep.

Dianne

Hundreds of people gathered for the grand opening celebration of Sylvia's Café. In standing formation folks engaged in heated discussions on politics, the latest defense strategy on the O. J. trial and who was making deals with whom—shaking hands with the devil and dancing by the light of the pale moon. I recall a lot about that night, particularly the people I met. But what impressed me most, and consequently reverberated my psychological bent, turned out to have nothing to do with politics, the O. J. trial or even closing the deal that might have marked my future. It was a surprising encounter with a remarkably beautiful woman that may have resulted in changing my life forever!

When I first saw Dianne flowing gracefully through the crowded café, I was prompted by an unyielding veil of curiosity. The rhythmic motion of her hips and arms swinging in perfect harmony with my accentuated heartbeat, hurled my emotions into a cascade of sensual thoughts. An overwhelming sense of anxiety swept over me. Suddenly I found myself anticipating her every move. She sauntered by me smiling sweetly from lips shimmering the color of crushed cranberries, set against perfectly white teeth and skin coated in honey. I attempted to embrace the feeling while cuddling a chill, when engulfed by the crowd, I lost sight of her!

From behind me, I then heard a voice whisper softly in my ear... "You're very alluring." Circling around in my head like the sweet celestial tone of a guardian angel, compelling me with chords of eroticism and sensuality, I heard the charming voice again..."I'm Dianne," she said.

As I turned, our eyes locked as we stood in silence. Dianne's beauty extended beyond the obvious perfect balance of her features and long, luxurious hair. It was the warmth and compassion, portrayed in her

18

luminous gray eyes that moved me.

After moments of silence between us, coveting merely the sheer desire to explore the possibilities, I had no clue where to begin. The lights dimmed, and the band started to play; conversations drowned out around us. I could barely see her silhouette when she leaned in close to me and smoothed her hand across my chest.

"Are you alone," she asked.

I had no immediate response, so I replied merely to encourage her intentions. "Why do you ask? Are you?" I responded.

She didn't answer...

I followed Dianne through large groups of people onto the balcony. She pulled out a red pack of Roth-Handle cigarettes and casually invited me to join her...

"Are you married?" she asked, lighting her cigarette, then mine.

"I'm not sure," I told her. "I think so," and chuckled.

She again had no comment...

Dianne winked as she gently folded her hand in mine and led me to the rear of the café.

"Wait here!" she said.

I awaited anxiously, anticipating Dianne's return as night fell unusually dark for early evening. There were a few stars twinkling in the distance and a full moon that hung hauntingly in the sky. I was instantly reminded of what a friend once told me about full moons... "Beware!" he told me. "Unusual encounters occur during the peak of the full moon... And people do crazy things!" I recall, wondering if tonight might be one of those crazy full-moon encounters for me. I couldn't imagine nor could I wait.

I thought of a conversation I might have with Dianne when she returned.

What would I say...if? What would she say...if? If I were alone with her in her bedroom late at night, what would happen?

These questions unanswered, a voice surfaced in the darkness... "Miss me?" Dianne taunted.

She touched my face with short sweeps across the cheek. Her light gray eyes were huge with luster and her face roseate...

"Yes...I missed you!" I said.

19

The air filled with the redolent smell of Dianne's sweetness. She was all of what I might look for in a woman, I thought. She was beautiful, warm and gentle. She took my hand and together we walked to the outside of the café. We entered a small room situated near the rear entrance of the kitchen. The room was dark and eerie. I felt for the light switch, flipped it on but nothing happened. I could feel Dianne's closeness but couldn't see her until she lit a small candle and sharp images began dancing on her face and the walls around us. I could see the room was empty but for a long countertop, sink and mirrors along the wall...

"I love this place!" Dianne said, giggling and guzzling from a bottle of Boodle's British Gin. She wiggled herself upon the countertop and leaned against the mirrors. Her dress slid up to her thighs, and I could see she was bare underneath. My heart beat out of control. I became warm then chilled. Menacing devils began dancing all around us as the enthused flame flourished. Her eyes seemed wicked, like piercing pools of madness, and her smile broadened as she took another swig, then shoved the bottle to my lips.

"Drink this!" she beckoned.

Gin streamed from the corners of my mouth as I wondered what I should do next. A hot, burning sensation coated my throat then rushed directly to my head; endorphins released in multiples. I felt a tingling sensation throughout my body when her lips brushed along my neck. She nibbled at my earlobe, licked and sucked it. Then from nowhere, she yanked my head back and began raking gently through my hair with hands as soft as spun silk. I thought she would kiss me when she pulled me close to her, but instead she slapped me—playfully at first, and then with a *wham* she hit me harder, and I fell slightly backward. She pulled me to her, then licked my mouth.

I'm in for it now, I thought and became instantly cautious and frightened of this gorgeous creature...

"You're exquisite!" she whispered. "So delightful!" And I relaxed for the moment.

Dianne loosened her hair, and piles of it fell to her shoulders. She tugged at her dress, and it fell to her waist, exposing billowy breasts and tanned nipples.

"Pour the gin...all over my breasts!" she ordered, breathing heavily.

Her body quivered as I obeyed and emptied the contents of the clear liquid over her shoulders and watched it smooth down her huge, firm breasts, along the soft skin of her nipples.

"Suck them!" she commanded, and placed her nipples between my lips. I sucked and cuddled her breasts until her eyes widened with the intense color of assorted grays. She placed my hand between her legs.

"Feel it?" she cooed. "Feel the moisture...soft as velvet, huh?"

I was driven by some inner force unfamiliar to me but very compelling. I placed my fingers deep inside her, spreading them slowly as I moved up to her secret garden. She *was* wet and soft as velvet. She was right!

She moaned and groaned, then screamed out. "Deeper...Deeper... Deeper..."

Hot liquid flowed freely as I reached deeper and she screamed louder..."Yes...yes...more...yes!"

I covered her mouth with mine to quiet her, and she began sucking my tongue, panting and gasping for breath. She suddenly jumped from the countertop, and her dress fell to the floor. She stood nude above net stockings and spiked heels.

"Do you like me?" she asked curtly. Not waiting for a response, she turned her back, spread her legs in a triangle-wide position and leaned over the countertop.

I want this, I thought but didn't say a word. When she looked back at me, she had fire and lust in her eyes. She flung her hair back over her shoulder, and it fell savagely around her body. The menacing devils that danced on the walls, now mirrored the shadow of her naked image—a wild stallion ready to be mounted and tamed!

"Eat me!" she screamed. "Eat me!"

I wrapped my lips around her hot, steaming wetness—licking and sucking until she poured out like a waterfall. I spread her legs wider with the width of my hands, gathered her hair and squeezed. She turned and playfully smacked me. I smacked her back, lightly at first, then harder on her rump. Instinctively, I knew what she wanted. I smoothed my hands along her sides, took her breasts and cupped them softly, then squeezed gently. She began uttering short barks as I smacked her rump again and again until the imprint of my hand shown bright red on her buttocks. I grabbed her hair, yanked her to me and kissed her mouth passionately, shoving my tongue down her throat. She began to shake, out of control, begging and moaning in gibberish.

"Darling...honey is that you?" a voice called out.

The light from the corner street lamp shone brighter as the door opened wider and a soft breeze brushed in. The candle's flame flickered and died. When my eyes focused, I could see it was John...

"Honey...what are you doing?" he asked as he walked closer.

"Oh...Ugh...Ugh...John," was all I could muster.

John's mouth flew open as Dianne turned to cover her nude body. "Who is that?" she asked.

"Oh...didn't I tell you? I'm married. Dianne, this is my husband, John...John...meet Dianne!"

Billets-Doux

It was with passion and fully suppressed longing that Carla formulated the words cleverly faceted to a single shred of brown paper. *My darling,* she wrote, *I love you. I miss you terribly.* The words, written in desperation, were embraced by a yearning for the life she once knew and cherished, now served as only a memory buried deep in her thoughts.

Cape Cod was a wonderful place, she thought. She longed for its passionate crystal-blue lakes, magnificent boats and wealth gained through inheritances. She was part of an elitist group, who lived on their boats and piloted their own helicopters. Fishing was merely a backyard treat and fine eating prepared by specialty chefs.

Just months ago she sailed along the Hudson to Manhattan with the man she dearly loved, and he had proposed marriage. It was in the heat of passion, while making love on the boat, that they decided spring would be the ideal time. She planned invitations. Only her dearest friends would attend.

Her body ached with a torturous passion as she touched herself where she recalled the warmth of her lover's mouth—his lips sweeping across her body; his soft, subtle whispers, brushing by her ears; his kisses placed on her forehead; and loving fingers between her legs.

She closed her eyes and recalled the cool, crisp wind that blew from the east coast as fall fell on the horizon that day. Making love on the boat was the last thing she remembered. There were men on the landing, watching her and her lover make love. He stripped her naked with the help of the wind thrusting between her legs. He slid her body over the sternum, and she spread her legs, shaping her bottom nicely. A slight chill filled the air, and the cool crispness rode their rhythm. He lifted her legs and licked her length. He twirled her around and smoothed her bottom, slamming it down on his lap and twisted her in position. She churned and slid with gesturing movements up and down in his lap then twirled her bottom around and from side to side, fueling his tightness against her narrowed walls. The men watched and waited.

Every word dripped with anguish as she sat quietly on the little cot where she was being held captive and tried to recall how she had come to this godforsaken place. But her memory was clouded, surmounted only by the severity of the brutal cold against her frail body and the painful words she wrote...*My darling, I love you. I miss you terribly. I don't know where I am....*

Carla slipped into a deep state of melancholy and wept. A tiny light streamed through a small crack in a boarded-up window and a nearby lake reeked with the stench of dampness and corrosion. *This must be a place of abomination,* she thought. She heard the sound of anchoring boats against the rush of crates being hoisted and thrown on deck. In the distance, a heavily wooded area of weeds, broken limbs and bramble bush was covered with frost. An overwhelming feeling of desperation came over her. Tears flooded her eyes and trickled down her cheeks, onto the wrinkled brown paper. Shuffling footsteps echoed, pallid voices surfaced and night darkened the room...

Two men entered, slowly moving toward her, one carried bundles of cords, the other, a large flashlight. Carla was panic-stricken.

"Wow! She's beautiful," one man commented and flashed a glaring light...

"How did you find her?"

Scuffling feet rushed by the door, and an older man entered holding a blindfold.

The image of a tall, dark man popped in her mind. He was one of the men waiting at the docks and watching them make love on the boat. It was he who stood before her. She was sure of it now. He owned her and now lurked in the shadows of her mind.

"Tie her down," he ordered. "Not too tight...damaged goods bring little return!"

Carla's body was wrenched with pain as her wrists and ankles were bound and the blindfold placed over her eyes.

"Gag her, stupid!" the man bellowed. "And hurry it up."

Breathlessly, Carla begged for mercy. "Don't...please...Don't hurt

24

me. Please...don't hurt me!"

"Let me see her," the older man scoffed and waved his hand upward.

Lifting her dressing gown, the two men removed the ties from around her ankles and spread her legs for the man to see.

"Ahhhh...Yesssss! She is truly a prize. Turn her over!" he snarled.

Without hesitation, the men tossed Carla over.

"Oooooh!" the man slurped. "Nice...a piece of art...let's get to work!"

Uncontrollably, the man slivered over to Carla and smoothed his hand across her bottom.

"Ooooooh, girl," he said, "you'll bring a pretty penny."

The man paced, looked between her legs again and took a deep breath. He licked his lips and fondled her breasts in his mind then wiped his hand across his mouth.

The men left the room, securing the door tightly behind them.

Carla immediately rolled over and fell to the floor, wiggling and squirming. The ties slackened from her ankles as she continued to fidget and twist. A ray of hope fluttered in her gut when the ties around her wrists loosened. She removed the blindfold and focused briefly on the moonlight streaming brilliantly through the cracked window boards. Not even a breath was heard as she reached beneath the mattress, removed the letter and recited the words from memory...*My darling, I love you. I miss...*

Her suspension of thought, interrupted by the outline of a flashlight that hung by the door, was another ray of hope, she thought. Her heart pounded as she tiptoed across the concrete floor, grabbed the lamp and crouched down in the corner of the room, clinging to the words she wrote...*I am filled with thoughts of you, my darling. I cannot bear our separation. If you only knew how I long for you, how your memory is embedded in my heart. You are the light of my life, the nourishment of my soul. It seems a century since I last saw you. Given my ill luck and nearing the gates of despair, I would gladly turn away and accept my fate just to hear you say I love you once again...*

The rattle of footsteps disarmed her. Horrified, she crawled across the floor. A man entered and reached for the flashlight as Carla curled up behind the cot, shivering. The man scanned the room and saw her silhouette huddled in the corner and cautiously moved toward her. She was petrified. Her heart beat out of control as she covered her head.

"Don't hurt me...please don't..." she cried.

The man reached for her as she lay motionless, cold and weak. He gently lifted her head and placed her on the cot, covering her mouth with his hand. He stroked her torn clothing and smoothed his jacket over her chilled body. A feeling of anxiety rose within him at the sight of her supple breasts exposed through the sheerness of her torn dressing gown. Her fear and helplessness instantaneously endeared her to him, and he adored her for it. A pureness of heart and an over-whelming sense of compassion overcame him...

"I won't...." he whispered. "I won't...hurt you."

The man gently whisked the back of his hand across her face and along her body. His mouth became dry when her deep, brown eyes flashed at him in terror. With both hands, he blanketed the outline of her hair.

"I promise...I won't hurt you!" he assured her. "I dare not..."

The man's gentle touch and sincerity were consoling.

"Where am I?" she pleaded. "Why am I here?"

"Shhhhh...don't talk," the man whispered. "All you should know is that I am a friend, and I'm going to help you."

Carla nodded, clinging to a grievous desire to be safe and back home with the man she dearly loved...

"Oh! Thank you," she exclaimed. "Thank you..."

"I'll be back," the man reassured her. "Don't worry."

Carla's lips parted slightly, not quite a smile, as he smoothed his hand along the top of her thighs and tenderly touched her hand.

"I promise...I'll be back...soon."

As he left, Carla cuddled the man's jacket close to her body and lay motionless. She was momentarily bathed in his lingering scent—a sweet aroma, strong and forceful, yet passionate and gentle. But her senses were filled with the memory of the man she truly loved, waiting for her return. The vision of their lovemaking flushed her mind as she clung desperately to the moment and dozed off with thoughts of the words she would write, when she awakened...*My life, so far away from you, is empty of all substance, and my existence lonely. I would anxiously count the days until we, at last, will be together again to share the divine love created between us, if only I knew when that day would come. Until then, my darling, the reality of my love for you can only be measured in exponential form, and that in itself falls short of its true magnitude—boundless and eternal. For you are the nourishment of my spirit and my only strength...*

Hours passed before Carla opened her eyes and saw the man had returned and was sitting beside her.

"I've brought you something to eat," he whispered.

Carla raised her head and stared at him with pitied eyes. She was moved by his charming and compassionate face, his passion and caring smile. She embraced his loving essence as he lay quietly beside her and spoke softly... "You're in danger. Listen to me carefully. I'm getting you out of here but first I must have a plan."

Resigned to his sincerity and the sound of commitment in his voice, Carla relaxed, nodded and smiled sweetly. He smoothed her soft brown hair against her face.

"You're very beautiful," he said. "What is your name? I am sure you are sadly missed."

"I am Carla," she answered.

"We must move quickly," the man said. "I'll explain later...The ties, Carla...where are the ties?"

Carla pointed to the floor beside the cot.

"I'll have to replace these." he said. "Just for a while..."

"If they come back, you should..."

Carla, overcome by her emotions, embraced and kissed him and passively held out her wrists.

"I'll return soon...I promise," he said and knotted the ties around her wrists.

"Who are you?" Carla muttered.

"Benjamin..." the man said. "Just, Benjamin..." and left the room.

Carla was full of anticipation. Butterflies flickered beneath her belly. She thought of Benjamin fondly, but wished soon, that she would be with the man she truly loved. It was a real possibility now, she thought. Mindful, she continued the words she would write to him...

I am left with little else but your name on my lips and your vision in my thoughts. I am confused with anguish and wracked with despair at the real-

ization that our separation is still in its infancy. How could fate be so cruel as to keep two people apart who so desire to be together? It is truly unbearable! Yet, I cannot change the present, therefore, I must live for the future. I now know that I must overcome my anguish and subdue my feelings of despair. This, I will attempt to do with the help of the love that binds our hearts across the miles that separate us. There are things in life that are inevitable; I am powerless to control them....

As she formulated the words, Carla realized that somehow it may not be her lover, miles away awaiting her return she was thinking about. It was the man with the compassionate eyes named Benjamin—the man with passion in his heart and a gentleness in his touch.

It was nearly dawn when Benjamin returned. Carla lay awake, waiting. He sat beside her and stroked her ankles and wrists, removing the ties. The taste of anticipation excited her. Not knowing what he would do next, her eyes fluttered and closed calmly. Benjamin placed a warm drink to her lips. The taste of sweet milk and honey soothed her. She offered no resistance when he slid down along her body and lay closely beside her. She could feel his strength of presence and unwavering devotion and completely relaxed—safe and protected with him.

"We must move quickly," he whispered. "Finish your milk, and we'll leave right away. Here, take these..."

Carla began undressing as he placed the clothing beside her. He watched her silhouette lay nude under the light of the pale moon, now streaming through the boarded window. Helplessly, he stroked her body with his eyes. She peeled off her dressing gown, and he envisioned his tongue against the flat of her stomach, lingering there and sliding along her silken thighs. His heart raced at the sight of her swelled breasts and perked nipples, arousing a deep note of eroticism within him. A sense of affinity swept over him.

He rubbed her breasts and softly kissed and caressed them. She felt his hardness against her thighs and took him in her hands and fondled him. She snuggled her head in the nap of his neck and lay still. He kissed her forehead, then the soft curvature of her shoulder, along her nipples and rested his head in the swelling of her breasts and suckled.

She began to shiver.

"It's very cold in this wilderness," he said. "These will keep you warm."

"You're very sweet," she said, as he helped her pull on her sweater and kissed her forehead.

"I've brought warm pants and a jacket for you, too..."

He looked at her, cherishing her loveliness when she exposed a bareness that touched an ideal place of comfort in him. With quivering wholesomeness, she arched the flat of her back as he stroked her body. She was wet, warm and willing...

"Hurry, put on the jacket," he said. "We must go!"

The thought of leaving this godforsaken place was a good thing, Carla thought, but the thought of leaving Benjamin was not. Her heart was heavy, torn and confused. She wanted to hold him close and passionately kiss his lips, lick him all over, run her fingers through his hair, rip at him, tear at him, welcome him and love him, all in the same moment. She was racing with lust, festering with passion and filled with a hurting sensation that rose deep within her. She envisioned his pulsation inside her fancy, stroking and sweltering beneath her.

The visualization of heated passion wrapped her body with warm delight. Swarming juices flowed between them as her legs and thighs cloaked his body. He entered her with a charming smoothness and slowly eased upward into her passion. She parted her legs and lay calmly. He stroked her, cuddling her fancy with peaceful, rhythmic lunges, thrusting her into a rush of tenderness. She was overtaken, meshed in the cradle of his arms. He rocked her with slow, even strokes. His tongue licked her neck, slid down along her plump breasts and found her nipples. He suckled them quietly and gently, pulling with succulent slurps, his tongue traveled along her body and found her navel and encircled it. He reached deeper within her sweet swelling and sheer desire imparted her willingness, and they flowed with each rhythm.

Her body rippled beneath his as he pressed against her belly and lingered there, searching for her feminine fountain with his fingers. He slipped his tongue inside her and spread her softness, slowly peeling pools of petals, releasing her passion. She pulled him between the chasm of her breasts, and he surged and gyrated. A rumbling orgasm rose within him as she took him in her mouth and clasped her lips around his hardness. Her mouth felt the heat looming from his throbbing pulsation and the intense strength of force from his loins. She thrust him spiritedly in her mouth. A spool of orgasms gushed between them, jolted by the hot exchange. It was wonderful, she thought.

"Let us go!" he urged. "We have little time..."

Carla could not bear the thought of ever being without him. The truth was in his eyes, and it told her he would never leave her. Her body surged with enchantment as his eyes revealed a pureness of heart and a precious love for her. She sighed a calm relief, knowing that this was true love and formulated the final words to her lover miles away, in thought only...

I have left you, my beloved. May the memory of my love follow and comfort you always. If you only knew how much I loved you, how essential you have been to my life. You will remain embedded in my heart—your soul to my soul. Je t'aime! Je t'aime! Je t'aime!

Au revoi, my beloved, Carla.

Hand in hand, Carla and Benjamin raced outdoors. Dawn spread its wings over the wilderness, and the sky opened up to them. Benjamin looked at Carla with love and smiled. He knew, just as she did, it was wonderful.

Bonita

"Get naked," the dominant lover growled, and Bonita knew she had better do so quickly. Stripped naked, she fell to her knees, immersed in the sound of Serolod's voice. Like doves tweaking in her head and the poignant howl of a lioness in heat, she was coiled with complacency. She slid her long, fiery-red hair over to one shoulder, bowed her head gently and accepted the gold-studded collar clasped firmly around her neck.

An imposing dark figure stood erect in the doorway, clutching his throbbing rivulet. Bonita watched and waited as the tall, dark man tightened his oversized fingers around the shaft of his pulsation and began slowly sliding up and down, until he reached a flow of hot semen. Multiple explosions seared throughout her body. The intensity proved overpowering, surrendering her effortlessly helpless. She breathed deeply, preparing for the conviction of her prowess and unleashed her passion, relinquished her soul, and sex slave became her name.

"Where is your mind?" Serolod snapped with lust in her eyes and pointed to the wild bush piled between her legs. "Eat me!"

Bonita resigned to her basic animal instinct and situated her head submissively between Serolod's legs, and the delicate gorging began.

The sweet smell of jasmine and heather spiraled the air as hot liquid covered her lips. The statuesque man watched intently from across the room, positioned comfortably in a large wicker chair as a towering ceiling fan swirled overhead and cooled the room.

The naked man advanced with the motion of Serolod's finger. His thick body swayed from side to side in perfect motion with his hardened elongation. He approached Bonita and immediately mounted her. His movements were exact, his delivery deliberate as he stroked her curvaceous body with slow, rhythmic motion. His hardness reached deep inside her swelling, parting her wider and wider with each gyration. He

31

licked her dark, erect nipples; she moaned as tears ran down her cheeks, onto her shoulders. Her back arched with an orgasm that began rolling deep inside her. A smooth modulation and continual withdrawing kept her heart pounding. Like an erupting volcano, a massive stream of hot lava exploded from the man, and Bonita unlocked a spastic orgasm. Serolod wrenched the man's pulsation from Bonita and began rubbing it with jasmine oil, then plunged his oily, bronzed lovelock into Bonita's tiny tan bottom.

"Give it all to her," she shouted. "All of it!"

The sound of Serolod's voice was like a breath from hell—a driving force that commanded Bonita's very soul. She gazed into Serolod's eyes with sheer subserviency, a wild lust, pitied with desire, hopelessly drawn into her spell.

"I want you, Serolod," she cried. "I want you...now!"

With a wave of Serolod's hand, the eager man, strapped a ten-inch love toy around Serolod's body and patiently looked on. Serolod enter-ed Bonita, plunging with a labor of love, laced with warmth and pur-pose.

"Oh...yesssss! That's what you want. Isn't it, love dove?"

Bonita smiled and bowed her head. She had not known such ecsta-sy, except perhaps in a fantasy-filled moment, sitting behind her desk at the local library, or sneaking a peek at a passage from a new erotica book that she had just shelved. She might have dared to explore the other side of her sexuality before now, but perhaps it could only have been possi-ble here, in this place, with this exotic partner that she could have tread the annuls of her sexuality, and done so completely removed from real-ity. Bonita sighed, lost in the enchantment of Serolod's intrigue, expressed by a compelling fire portrayed in her eyes and a heightened sexual intensity of sheer sensuality.

"Where is your mind?" Serolod charged.

Bonita's secret place was serene and comfortable as Serolod gyrated and swirled her body, plunging deeper and deeper, massaging and taunt-ing her.

"You love it...don't you? You sweet slut...don't you? How much of this do you want? Bend over...and let me have it!"

Bonita wailed with conviction. "Yessssss...Yes! You're my purest passion."

Lost in her own lust, she began to whimper as Serolod continued to taunt...

"You sweet lamb...You're mine...aren't you?...You're my sex slave."

Bonita screamed out..."Yesssss...I belong to you. Take me...Lick me!"

Serolod sucked and licked, and suckled and coddled as Bonita cried tears of joy, licked her lips and panted.

"On your knees," Serolod glowered, and positioned Bonita to be entered from the rear.

"Please...please...please...take me," Bonita begged. "I want you. I want you!"

Serolod shoved into Bonita's opening with a twirling movement, creating a sloshing rhythm that closed the sanction reserved only to the most secret corners of her mind. With final remittance, Serolod touched Bonita's true hot spot, measuring the heightened state of her bliss and moved along her inner walls, deepening her commitment to explore. Bonita's body became limp, barely able to withstand the degree of intensity and began trembling out of control. Her body and soul became the substance of all her erotic desires, deepened by a passionate commitment to her sexual prowess and curiosity. The softness of her supple breasts was filled with a torrid fire as she awaited Serolod's next charge.

She was held in awe by Serolod's compelling voice and mesmerized by her own transformation.

Serolod snatched the man's love handle and shoved it into Bonita's mouth.

"Suck this!" she demanded, then pushed her fingers deep inside Bonita and shouted, "Suck that big black..."

Bonita was on fire as she slurped and licked the head of the man's lock. Serolod's fingers slipped upward to her passion, gently stroking and pulling. The man slowly inched down Bonita's mouth, moaning with fulfillment. A waft of creamy lava streamed from Bonita's lips as Serolod retrieved her fingers from her hot wetness and licked them and pointed between her legs. Bonita quickly thrust her tongue between Serolod's legs and licked along its fine, wet creases. Serolod looked down at Bonita and smiled with crazed eagerness..."Do...do it...do it..."

Bonita rotated her tongue along Serolod's plump edges and Serolod howled in lust... "Oooooh...you sweet lamb. Yesssss...yessss...do it!"

Tears welled in Serolod's lust-filled eyes as she grabbed Bonita's pursed mouth and passionately kissed her.

"I like it," she conceded. "I like it!"

The man pulled Serolod's drenching, hot body away from Bonita and piled rows of pillows beneath her groin. He massaged himself over her body, until he hardened, slapped her on the bottom and entered her from behind. Massaging and lunging, quickly created a slurping sound that grew louder and faster with each thrust.

"Yesssss...yesssss...yessss! Perk it up," he howled. "Turn it loose!"

Serolod cried out with passion as Bonita glistened with joy, spawned by the eclipse she felt in Serolod's comfort zone. Bonita cherished the thought and began massaging Serolod's breasts—sucking, pulling and rubbing. Serolod drew Bonita's mouth to her, kissed her gently and whispered the words she longed to hear...

"Come to me, my love...my dove. Come to me...."

Bonita awoke in a pool of sweat, alone and covered by her own sweetness and the lingering sound of Serolod's voice...

"Come to me, my love...my dove. Come to me again, soon."

Bonita made a mental note.

Cowboy

Cowboy wrapped the thickly knotted rope three times around his right gloved hand, secured his wide-brimmed hat with his left and postured himself for the mighty fury expected from an agitated bull whose testicles were harnessed for the event but much too tight. He buckled his knees around the torso of the bull, shook his head to clear his thoughts and prayed for endurance. Smoke hurled through Freighter's flared nostrils as he scuffed and huffed, bobbed and weaved and demonstrated his fierce power and anger. Cowboy, attempting some form of psychological control over the bull's mighty dominance, yanked the bull rope twice, pounded his thumb over the rope in place, then nodded to the gatekeeper.

Freighter dug his powerful front hooves deep into the dirt, eager to begin his belligerent bull's dance and flew across the arena, bucking and charging.

"Freighter weighs more than three thousand pounds, folks!" the rodeo announcer began. His voice echoed throughout the arena..."A monstrosity of a bull, he's a raving maniac!"

Freighter hunkered down, lowered his horns to the ground, then leaped high in the air, popping his head from side to side. He kicked back twice, heaved his forceful hooves to the ground and propelled himself forward.

"Freighter's plenty ferocious," the announcer shouted.

"He's got personality...personality like a freight train!"

Freighter took an abrupt swerve to the left, a quick spin to the right and plummeted his rear end in the air. With the mighty force of his front hooves, he backed up then kicked off. Thousands of spectators stood twirling their hats in the air. Whistles flooded the arena from every direction.

"Cowboy's the favorite among bull riders," the announcer proclaimed.

"He's a bull-rider's rider...a real cowboy...been ridin' bulls since he was seven."

The crowd cheered as Cowboy's neat, close-to-the-ground figure and powerfully cut arms and thighs postured for combat. He needed control over the mighty Freighter to win this bull-riding championship. It was an enormous feat, he thought. But he was feeling high on the hog and determined to take him out.

"Cowboy's a hero back home," declared the announcer. "He looks real good out there, so far. The arena's full of folks today...looks like a good majority are cowboys and bull riders. They're here from all over the country to witness Cowboy seize the challenge...

"I see Bill Pickens is out there...You all know Bill Pickens. Holds that first bull-riding world cup championship, back in the fifties...Cowboy's got plenty support out there today!"

The whistling and cheering swelled.

"Two seconds..." the announcer counted.

Cowboy tightened his thighs around Freighter's wide, muscular frame, flexed his chest muscles and locked in his shoulders, attempting to hold down the grit-spirited fire that was surfacing beneath him.

"Only one other guy ever rode Freighter more'n three seconds," the announcer affirmed. "Billy Ray Thunder! Another prime-time rodeo champ...been head bronco in these parts for about three years now...Unfortunately, he's not here with us today, folks...had a real bad accident back in November...his last ride out.

"Here's to you, Billy Ray...Hope to see you back real soon!"

Cowboy's legs jolted away from the bull's body and plummeted in the air. He slid down along the bull's side as Freighter skidded and took an abrupt jerk to the left, a quick spin to the right, twisting and turning like a towering tornado. Cowboy pulled himself up with powerfully cut arms, yanked on the bull rope and rode the rhythm of the bull's fierce dance.

"What a ride!" exclaimed the announcer. "What a ride!"

Cowboy tried to concentrate on the fourteen thousand dollars he would win for riding this mighty monster for just eight seconds. But

36

eight seconds seemed like a lifetime to him...

"Four seconds..." the announcer screamed... "He's hangin' in there, folks!"

Cowboy's body became rigid as Freighter surged through the air and tossed Cowboy in opposition with his rhythm. Disarmed for a moment, Cowboy landed on the bull's massive back with a tremendous blow, and attempting to contain himself, corralled the mighty force of Freighter's anger. He relaxed his back, fastened his lower body firmly to the bull and yanked on the rope for dear life. His left arm dangled in the air as Freighter took a quick turn to the left, a swift curve to the right, lunged and kicked out backward.

"It's gonna take some real skill to win this one," the announcer confirmed. "This bull means business! Cowboy's being tossed around out there pretty bad...Matter of fact, this is his first national competition. He's got to earn this one!"

Freighter shoveled dirt with all fours, jolted forward with an exhilarating plunge, and Cowboy was instantly stunned. He thought about the tantalizing stories he told the cowboys back home that were so compelling that his reputation stood on them. He had to live up to the stamina and endurance he claimed. Bull riders would gather from far and wide just to hear Cowboy tell his tales about exactly how to win over a bull...

"Bull riding takes true grit," he told them. "Takes skill, concentration...and a real winning strategy...When I'm ridin' that bull...I hold on to that sucker, till he hunkers down... till it feels like I'm ridin' my best girl...Then, I slap that bottom, grab them hips with my thighs and lock down...I stretch them knees and tighten them thighs and dig in...Then I listen for them huffs and puffs...and when my groin starts to poppin'...I let them juices flow...And ride 'em, cowboys...ride 'em...That's how it's done...That's how you do it...Tame a bull...Win a sweetie...Ride 'em, cowboys, like it's your last bull ride...like your last roll in the hay with your best girl...like never before!"

Cowboy captured the ears and curiosity of cowboys and bull riders, week after week, until his audiences spanned more than four counties. He told the same story, expanding each time—adding a little more flavor, a little more drama and a few more lies.

Cowboy slapped his thighs, jumped up and down, and the cowboys squatted around the fire, chanting in rhythm...

"Let's round 'em up...that's how we do it...just how it's done... Tame a bull...Win a sweetie...Ride that bull like it's your last bull ride...like your last roll in the hay with your best sweetie...Let's round 'em up...that's how we do it...just how it's done..."

Cowboy soon became a hero among the bull riders and cowboys. The more lies he told, the more they loved him for it. He cornered their enthusiasm week after week, sometimes months before a competition, and told his tales with great enthusiasm, visual antics and always with claims of victory.

"See...I'm ridin' my best sweetie girl," Cowboy would explain—with arms extended, knotted fists and swinging his body back and forth, like a pendulum.

"See? I ride 'em, cowboys. Yaaaaaaw...Whooooo...Forward, backward, faster and faster...Ride 'em, cowboys!"

Cowboy slapped both thighs, jumped in the air and hollered, landing with a jolting bang, spun around, jumped up again and came down swiveling his hips from side to side.

"Round and round...rotate that direction...and rock that body... In and out...and round about!" Cowboy crooned, as the cowboys joined in with clowning antics.

"Let's round 'em up...that's how we do it...just how it's done...Tame a bull...Win a sweetie."

Cowboys and bull riders slapped their thighs, twirled their bodies and jumped up and down as Cowboy pivoted in a circle and slapped his bottom.

"See? You slap that bottom...tighten them thighs...lock in them knees and rock that movement...and claim the victory...Ride that bull...Ride that sweetie... Listen for them hollers and rock that body with do-right motion...Hit that reset button...And...ride 'em, cowboys... Ride!"

"Five seconds..." the announcer screamed, as Cowboy plunged toward the upper torso of the bull's twisting and jerking body and almost flipped over his head. He hollered in sheer terror; his body was racked with pain. He loosened his thighs, grasped the bull rope, tight-

38

ening his fist around it. He struggled with the rope, pulled himself up in place and held on for dear life. Cowboy leaned back and anchored his body. Freighter scuffed and huffed, bucked and jerked, touted his head from side to side and kicked and grunted. He blew out steam from both nostrils. Cowboy slid forward and Freighter went down with a vicious plunge and kicked back.

"Cowboy's holdin' on...What a bull rider!"

Cowboy grabbed the rope, pulled up and locked down his thighs, bolstering his body back on the bull. His groin popped when the bull reared back, then dropped his front end. Cowboy plummeted forward, almost hitting the ground, and the bull came up on front hooves, his back end still twisting in the air. It was now Cowboy needed his winning strategy...

He jabbed her opening with a love force that touched her bottom instantly. She felt the impact of his surge as he boned the gristle out of her. She panted when he hit her reset button and mauled her with the strength and force of the mighty bull within him. He romped and roared, threw her legs high in the air and yanked and snatched. He swelled with each stroke then drilled his rise right out of her and quickly shoved it in her mouth. With a jolting zest and vivacious exertion, he savored the stratagem and maneuvered the effort.

The bull beneath him ripped through the air, kicked out his hind legs and arched his neck, dropping his horns close to the ground. He kicked back will full-forced energy and charged.

Cowboy gyrated and pivoted, then swiftly threw his girl on her stomach. He held her hands high above her head, snapped her back end in place and narrowed his knees on either side of her body. He entered her, suspended in the air, slammed her body down and slid his rock-hardened elongation deep within her and locked down. His thighs tightened around her body, and he narrowed his knees as he plunged deeper. The thrilling and thrusting sensation warmed her entire body from head to toe, and she loved him for it!

"To the left...to the right...Oh, boy! " the announcer screamed. "Freighter's flinging Cowboy out there...like a rag doll!"

Cowboy slapped her bottom and stroked her neck, holding her head firmly on either side with both hands. With a mighty force, he gyrated and plunged and pulled and twirled and ripped at her insides with luminous gristle, swelling with each gyration.

"Six seconds..." the announcer yelled. "Whatcha think, folks...is Cowboy gonna make it?"

Cowboy's chaps flapped in the wind, his right hand held fast around the bull rope, his left hand flinging and twirling in the air.

His sweetie screamed and hollered and scuffed and huffed and perked up, targeting his position. Cowboy jabbed into her with a mighty fierce conviction, gyrating and plowing. She purred with sensations, crawling through her veins with pestilential measures and escalated his sensual force. "Ohhhhh, Cowboy..." she panted. "I love it. Give me all you got!"

Cowboy pulled himself up on the bull; his arms weak against the rise of Freighter's anger. He cringed, knowing he was no match for the mighty power of Freighter.

"Just a few seconds," the announcer called out. "Hang in there, Cowboy!"

Cowboy exploded with a ravaging pain that riveted his body and tightened his muscles and locked down with resounding quickness.

"Yaaaaaw...Whooooo...I love it!" he hollered.

"Ooooooh...let it go...girl!"

"Seven seconds," the announcer shouted.

Freighter abruptly jerked his body to the right, kicked out all fours and landed on the ground, digging in his hooves. Suddenly with a leap and twist in midair, he jerked his body to the left, to the right, twirling and twisting and gyrated circles.

Cowboy threw his girl on her side, threw up her legs and pierced her with gyrating circles and continued to plunge. The instant sloshing and wading proved his strategy was tight, his formation perfect and rhythm right with hers. He turned into a bucking bronco and rode her like it was his last bull ride...his last roll in the hay with his best sweetie. He slung her body over, held her down on both sides of her body, then propped her legs high over her head and hunkered down. He moved fast, rotating his body with ferocious strokes and listened for the screams and hollers she would discharge. Like sweet celestial chimes to his ears, her screams riveted his body with trembling true grit. He surged deeper and frayed her. She screamed and hollered, suspended in ecstasy.

Cowboy's adrenaline flowed freely as his muscular body began to sweat profusely and foaming juices heaved from his mouth. The intensity proved exhilarating, yet overwhelming.

"Eight seconds..." the announcer screamed. "Look out...Billy Ray Thunder!"

"Yaaaaaaw...Whoooooo!" Cowboy yelped.

With a burst of potency and vigorous energy, Cowboy shot out like a bull with convulsions—an explosion that popped in his groin and seeped into his brain. His girl began to shake out of control. Firecrackers blew off in her head, cracking and popping with sensual sensations that instantaneously seared throughout her body.

Freighter threw Cowboy, sweeping him clear across the arena. Cowboy hit the ground, slid six feet, drudging up a pile of dust, and Freighter charged after him. The dust cleared. Cowboy laid on the ground with blood trickling down his face. He rolled over in the dirt, barely escaping the path of Freighter's fury as two clowns rushed in the arena. Cowboy hurled himself over the railing and fell to the ground. Freighter bucked and danced in circles, then kicked against the railing with powerful blows from his back hooves.

"Wait a minute, folks...I think Cowboy's hurt!"

The clowns rounded up Freighter, and Doc Collins rushed toward Cowboy. Freighter bucked and charged and ran through the opened gate, blowing and kicking.

The crowd cheered and stomped on the stands. Whistles and claps were heard throughout the arena. Cowboy's adrenaline was racing high, his testosterone running low. Disoriented, bordering delirium, he looked out at the spectators and impulsively began waving his hat.

"Looks like Cowboy's waving to the crowd," the announcer shrilled. "He's alright, folks! Looks like we got ourselves a new bull-ridin' champ."

Eight seconds lit up the scoreboard.

"...He's done it, folks...he's done it...in eight seconds flat. Cowboy's a winner!"

The crowd cheered and whistled and stamped their feet on the stands, threw their hats into the arena and shook their fists high in the air.

"Here's to you, Cowboy," the announcer shouted. "Congratulations!"

Cowboy jumped straight up, threw his hat on the ground and hollered and danced in circles.

"Yaaaaaw...Whooooo!" he howled.

"Let's round 'em up...that's how we do it...just how it's done..." Cowboy's girl tore herself away from the spectators stand and raced across the arena. She could hardly retain herself as she jumped in Cowboy's arms and squeezed and hugged him. She smiled sweetly, grinning from ear to ear and waved to the crowd.

"I felt it, Cowboy," she purred. "I felt the explosion..."

Cowboy jumped straight up. He could barely contain himself, anticipating his next gathering with the boys back home, to tell them just how he did it...

"Just when that bull was 'bout to throw me...buckin' and kickin' and snarlin'...I grabbed them ropes, locked in them knees and buckled down...I got eight seconds...see? I know I gotta ride that bull...So, I ride 'em like it was my best sweetie! I feel that big bang comin'...I just been waitin' on that, see! Yaaaaaw...Whooooo! I ride 'em, cowboys...ride that fear...ride that adrenaline. And let it go, boys...Just let it go...and ride! Ride them firecrackers in your head...Ride them pops in your groin, like sweet chimes to my ears...like a sweetie purrin' sweet nothin's in my ears...I ride 'em, cowboys...I ride 'em like it was my last bull ride...like it was my last roll in the hay, with my best sweetie. Let's round 'em up...that's how you do it...just how it's done..."

Dark Desire

It's eerie the way we breathe in unison and our hearts beat in perfect harmony. Our bodies are synchronous, vibrating within the same resonance. Our souls merge as we shadow the exchange of each other's movements. I see through dreamy eyes, clustered with soft, sultry images. A tiny tattoo of a salamander is perfectly placed on your pubic mound. You are an exotic creature, spun from the goodness of time, and your enchanting languor of thought shines brilliantly even through artful play. You are cunning as a snake, exact in your movement and command my lust with clockwork precision...

Known only to those with vision, these stories unfold in figments of imagination as you gracefully evolve and I rest comfortably in the curvature of your secret place. My tongue caresses gently along your soft petals and moistened creases of sweetness. Within your folds, I gently dart in and out with ease, and you comfort me perfectly when I do. I crawl along your smooth, silky body like a rivulet and glide along your walls. Your juices surrender sweetly, flowing from petals that open like a flower in bloom—so willingly and completely.

A dark desire flows through my veins with a rise of obsession that buries me deeper in your enchantment. Your love covers me with an essence that gushes like a waterfall, forever yielding, forever filling me with fruit of passion.

Our union breathes words of passion....

"Lick me, my love," you whisper. And I do, tasting and sucking as you reach for the inside my thigh.

"Come deeper to me," you say, and with revealing eyes..."I've got more for you," you mutter. "More love than you'll ever desire...new love...deep love...just for you."

I release all inhibitions, responding... "I love you...I love you...I love you!"

You reply in perfect harmony with my purest desire, and I am total-ly lost in your lust. I express my love with whimpering barks and smiles of joy and in my helplessness, promise to love you forever. You release for me, the way I like it, all over my face, repeatedly and with earnest. I moan with passion, then roar with strength of the conviction, knowing I am safe within the sweetness of your love.

"Yes...Yes...Yessssss..." I howl.

"Scream louder!" you say, and I do, with a scowl of retreat pleading for more...

"Oh, my love...My love...I am yours, unconditionally. Give me more. Do as you please...I am yours."

"Suck me," you say, and I do, parting your thighs, slowly entering your flower, licking, soothing and tranquilizing your body.

With words of hunger, you say the sweetest things to me...

"I want you...goddess of love. You will forever pirouette in my soul."

I gently squeeze you and cherish the way you feel between my fin-gers, your firmness, your stretch, your reach within my swelling. You nibble and caress my nipples with tiny bites, teasingly, sucking and stroking gently. I guide your surge inside me.

Your movement spawns an eclipse in me.

"Oooooooh...I like it!" I surrender, and you cuddle me.

"Do you like this?" you ask.

"I do...I do...I do..." I purr as my body shivers and welcomes the release of my transgressions.

I pant helplessly and cry out..."More...more...more..." And await our next frame of exchange.

In my dark desire, I am filled with all that I know—flourished with the hunger of buried passions, soar with the force of the universe and await with bated breath for the rush that accompanies the overwhelm-ing scent that encompasses our final outpour. I resign to your every wish, your every desire, given willingly, a surrender of all things. As our union is secured with the certainty of love, I entertain your most frail thoughts and frivolous whims.

Even in your thoughtlessness, you spur the sweetest emotion in me.

You playfully slap me and tell me to beg your forgiveness.

I have long awaited this...

"Please, my love, please forgive me," I plead, as you bubble with delight and bow my head in resignation to your secret place.

Your legs open to my pleasure, and I rush in where only lovers dare tread.

"More?" you question.

"Yes...oh, yes!" I say, and you fray me with words that breathe my desperation.

"Beg for it!" you exclaim.

And I love you for it!

In my dark desire, orgasms rush to my pleasure.

"Please..." I beg. "Please, my love..."

In the darkest realm of my mind, I know that I must implore your forgiveness, for surely I am deserving and have wronged...

"...For whatever I have done...for my deepest and darkest uncensored selfish thoughts...all my foul deeds. Please...forgive me!"

The aroma looming from your secret garden claims the essence of my soul's desire. I can never love another as I do you, or know another as I do you. No one enchants me the way you do, or adores me so.

You say the sweetest things when I rest my head in the roundness of your breasts and hover there, suckling and cuddling.

"I love you," you say, "with all my heart," and I am lured by your certainty.

When I am alone, I fantasize only of you, and in my fascination, visualize you in the most provocative positions, captivating an image that no one else can see or feel. I think of the lust that will exude from my loins and once again, drawn helplessly into the delight.

Sometimes, I feel foolish, overwhelmed by the enchantment and humiliated by the vision. But even so, my captivation with your charm is a decided increase in my social stature, for I am without will but for yours. I yield to the dark desire, again and again captivated by the soft, sultry images, even though it is only as a virtual voyeur.

Daring Innuendo

I woke up with my lover last night after one of our heated sexual encounters, and by some macabre twist of fate realized that our labored fruits of passion had lost their luster. I felt this uncontrollable urge to vent and move on. So, I'm doing what I always do when a relationship loses its sex appeal. I cut off my hair and shave my pubic mound. But this time, I'm crafting a little heart-shaped figure, with pretty detailed edges with the cluster of hair between my legs. I want to remember to use my head and not my heart in future relationships. In short, I'm performing a ritualistic exorcism of sorts, an ongoing psychological condition my therapist calls compulsive behavior disorder. Frankly, I call it expressing myself. See, removing unwanted hair eliminates the possibility of any psychological venom that may be lingering. Plus, it appeals to my animalistic nature, by adding a decided boost to my next adventure. I'm also, spraying a little extra Boucci behind my ears, my knees and especially between my legs. I'm on the prowl. I've decided to get laid today.

Meet China. He's my newest flame—highly sexed, softly spoken and built like a compact brick house. China offers all the pleasures of a man in demand just waiting to be challenged to deliver. He has other qualities, like good looks, nice personality and great smile. But let's face it! It ain't his handsome looks, or pleasing personality that intrigues me. It's his long, hard handle that's got my attention. Needless to say, China has gotten under my skin and frankly, deep in the cut of things.

Our relationship began with sex. I first noticed China during one of his grueling, heated workout sessions at Gold's gym. I sauntered by him, with measured, stealthy steps, throwing my hips from side to side and captured his attention. He smiled broadly, bordering a grin, and when our eyes met, transfixed in a stare, an amazing thing happened. His love lock seemed to jump out of his gym shorts to greet me. I started snickering, covering a beaming leer and mounted the leg extension machine.

I watched him closely as he placed a few hundred pounds of weights onto a barbell, lifted it up on his shoulders and slowly begin to squat. He let out a loud grunt from the weight of the barbell and his bulky thighs pumped to a huge bulge. His facial grimace expressed severe pain but I could tell he loved it when he threw the barbell to the floor, looked directly at me and grinned.

"Oooooh..." I began, as I opened and closed my legs against the force of the leg machine. I breathed deeply and progressively widened my legs with each execution.

His tongue extended as he squatted again.

"Oooooh! Oooooh..." I cooed.

He bit the bottom of his lip, smiled sweetly and added a few more hundred pounds to his already weighted-down barbell. I counted ten repetitions, when he let out a loud, elongated, bull-like sound and threw the barbell to the floor.

I poured out like a waterfall..."Oooooh...Yessssss!" I moaned, as I watched the sweat glisten over his muscular body, slowly slide down his hard, tanned chest and bead around his groin. He licked the sweat from his lips and squatted again. I became detached from embarrassment and shifted into entice gear. I sashayed by him and with an extended forefinger, beckoned him to follow me. Without conversation, he trailed me into the ladies' sauna area. No questions asked, no explanations required.

He stood before me like an anxious puppy. I locked the door and added water to the already steaming coals and slowly began peeling off my gear. I became warm and excited as butterflies flickered beneath my groin. I could feel his eyes bathing my body when I exposed soft perked raspberry nipples and sleek tanned skin, against a slim, hard body. His eyes widened with the sight of my heart-shaped pubic mound, and he licked his lips. I was feeling in control, proud and sexy as I slid onto the bench, slightly spread my legs and gave him a sneak preview. His tongue fell out of his mouth. He was pumped, I was plump...

China stripped his gym shorts, revealing a monstrous love lock that folded out like a hose. He pressed himself against my body, fully hardened, pulsating and firmly locked between my thighs. I tightened and squeezed, then took him in both hands and began massaging him. My heart beat out of control. His pulsation throbbed against the softness of his skin, and I was prompted to slide him into my mouth. I did, and he looked down at me with twinkling lust. I could feel the pounding of his heart through the sensation along the walls of my mouth...

"Want this?" he asked.

Oh, yeah! I can deal with this, I thought, but didn't answer him. Instead, I urged him deeper into my mouth.

"My name is China. What's yours?" he asked.

I didn't have time to answer all those questions. The smell of passion had filled my senses, and my loins ached. He grew bigger as I slid him deeper inside my throat. He was filled with moans of pleasure as I kissed, nibbled and sucked until his hardness became a vision of veins, and my comfort zone deliciously softened.

"Oooooh...baby...Yessss!" he screamed. "You're good! Aren't you, baby?"

Still, no answers, I continued to work him like a vacuum.

"I like it," he said. "I love it...I wanna be all up inside you...from top to the bottom, inside and out!"

He grabbed my body with a long, sweeping movement, picked me up and placed me on the bench. I was on fire! The thought of his warm tongue all over my body and tickling me deep inside threw my psyche into overdrive. I spread 'em. He reached for my pubic area with his tongue and with both hands, slowly opened and began suckling, slurping, nibbling and licking.

I was flowing with Niagra Falls, atop Mount Kilimanjaro. I was swaying with the leaning Tower of Pisa. I was Zena, queen of the jungle and Tarzan's Jane, all wrapped up in one. Tears flooded my eyes as I shivered with a riveting lust and multiple orgasms.

I was thinking about how unusual the name China is, when he entered me with a snug, elongated plunge. I encircled his movements with tightened legs and increasing measures. My head, not my heart, took over. I was not in love. I was in lust.

"Damn! I like it!" he whispered. "You feel good," and plunged deeper.

With focus on my feminine fountain, he reached a point of no return.

"Let me taste you..." he panted with enthusiasm.

I fell to the bench and opened my legs wide. He began sucking and licking as sweat mixed with passion—delicious, drenching and hot! He smoothed open my heart-shaped pubic mound with his hands, wiped the sweat from his brow and buckled his mouth between my legs. With sweeping licks and long, extended tongue, he feasted. I grabbed his head and pressed harder. His mouth perched, and his lips pursed. My nipples hardened with a torturous passion. I turned around and slung myself over the bench. Then with a riveting movement, he knelt down and slid himself deep inside me. I was sopping wet, he was rock hard. He never seemed to stop gliding upward toward my secret garden and with a driving force, reached home instantly. He turned me to the side, lifted my leg over his shoulder and entered me, screaming, "Oooooh, baby...you're so good. You're in control of this!"

I shook my head to clear the insanity as he pulled himself out, turned me around and placed me on the bench. He jerked open my legs and pierced my opening with a fast, shoving, forklike movement. I wrapped my legs around his hard, wet body and pulled him closer. He rammed and pulled in and out, faster and faster, until he unleashed a massive flow, and I poured out with multiple explosions.

I dressed, panting out of breath...

"See ya!" I said. "By the way, my name is Smokey," and left him standing there hot, wet and covered with my very own flavor of chocolate pudding.

Harumph!!!! Like I said...Meet China. He's my newest flame—softly spoken, highly sexed and built like a compact brick house—and incidently, the lay of the century.

Max

I could barely make out his hard outline when he closed the door behind me but I could see that Max was completely nude. His huge, bulky thighs, narrow waistline and thick massive chest became clear only when my eyes adjusted to the pitch blackness surrounding us. With the help of the tiny streetlight shining through the cracks in the shutters, I watched his statuesque silhouette flow like that of a Greek god. Max had muscles in places you would not believe...

Max and I had been the best of lovers for months. We met every Thursday, always at night and always in his little apartment off the beaten track of the main roadway. I tried to recall when he last took me in his arms and gently kissed me; but weeks had passed since our last encounter, and all I could remember was that I came to him every Thursday and stopped. I looked in his eyes, searching for the gentleness of his nature I had grown to expect but what I saw was an absence of composure situated deeply in his eyes, widened with rage and in a most peculiar way. They were like piercing pools of madness reflecting disharmony on the otherwise perfect features of his face. The bitterness I sensed in him frightened me. He began tearing at my clothes. His eyes were flashing as he ripped pieces of clothing from my body until I was completely nude. He lifted me high above his chest, kicked open the door to his bedroom, and threw me.

"You're mine," he shouted. "Mine...you hear me? Mine, whenever I want...You're mine!"

I landed so hard in the middle of his large antique bed that the springs echoed several times from the impact. He straddled my body and bound my wrists behind me. I felt something soft and fury trail along my backside and between my legs. I could no longer see the shadows of the trees reflecting from the tiny streetlight outside the window. I saw nothing, I was blindfolded. A thick aroma of wicked black cavendish blanketed the room. Intoxicated, drunk with panic or perhaps passion, I was jerked to my knees. His fingers began massaging between my legs, over my backside and along my spine. I could feel his well-formed hardness press against my rear and linger there. It was hot, thick and long. I wanted to scream out, but couldn't. I was gagged! I had never known Max to be like this. Our encounters had been hot, intense, even wild as lustful stolen fruits of passion can sometimes be, but never like this!

He loosened the ties that bound my wrists and pulled my head back with the weight of my hair. He fondled my breasts, caressed and squeezed my nipples until they hardened. He smacked my rear again and again, and my body ached with a kind of torturous passion on the verge of exploding, when his penis reached long and deep inside of me. Wedged firmly between my legs and kneeling behind me, he began pushing and pulling himself in and out...in and out...over and over... again and again, swelling inside me with each gyration.

With the continuous stream of hot liquid flowing between us, my body shook out of control. Dancing in my head was the sharp edge of an enthused flame that virtually compelled me to tears. I slipped away into a deep well of nothingness—a place where nothing mattered but the drenching multiple orgasms and inhumane ecstasy I was now entangled in with Max.

And then there was no more pain, no more shaking, no more tears. Sublime ecstasy took over.

Max tore off the feathered mask that blindfolded me and threw it across the room then ungagged my mouth. I was gasping for breath when he said something I wasn't quite sure of, but I think he said, "Plead for more...plead!"

So, I played along.

"Please, Max...please...I want more...I need more of you!"

But like a vulture, he was on top of me again, shoving himself inside me. He ran his tongue down my throat and sucked my tongue until it pained. And the movement began again... pushing and pulling...in and out...in and out...over and over...again and again. I had never known such orgasm, such ecstasy. He pulled himself out of me, got back into bed and piled rows of pillows beneath his head.

51

Rage rose within me as Max watched me search along the floor for my clothing, teary-eyed, confused and clueless. I found only fragments of what I had worn that night but I didn't care. In the paradise of love I had once known with Max, turned sadistic nightmare, I wanted out. My eyes focused on an object that had fallen from the bed during our episode. It was phallic-shaped, long and thick. Without forethought, I picked it up and threw it at him.

"Use this on yourself, you creep," I screamed. "How dare you!"

Bewildered, he jumped out of the bed and ran over to me. He held both of my arms and with trembling lips and pleading eyes, cried out, "I'm sorry. I...I'm so sorry." His arms were extended and an underlying expression of resignation was in his voice, "Don't go," he said. "... Please don't...I didn't...I...Please don't leave me!"

I took one last glimpse of Max before leaving and saw a sheer sense of frustration on his face. "Just like all the others," he mumbled. "...my wife...my girlfriend...my mother... you're leaving me!"

With black-feathered blindfold neatly piled away in my bag, I left apartment six that night, vowing never to return. I thought about John, Darron and Walter and all the others I didn't remember the names of, and deep down inside, I knew that Max would only join the plethora of men I had loved in some strange way. I would think of Max as I had all the others, a well-kept secret—a familiar feeling of quiet control. I would hold the memory of him deep inside me, only if my memory chose to serve me in that way. And if it unexpectedly reared its ugly head, I would have to say that it was crazy, but in a strangely provocative way, I liked it! I liked being submissive to Max. I did wonder why my warm and gentle lover had suddenly turned sadistic. I concluded that perhaps it had always been in him. Too bad, he had gone too far.

I would remember our last encounter as a fantasy that lived, a warm, quiet control like orchestrating an unrehearsed magnificent piece of music that surprisingly surfaced and lived. I must say, I was pleased with all the satisfaction that comes with a standing ovation and perhaps an even greater anticipation of our next encounter, if I dared!

Housemates

Evelyn howled from her bedroom door. "Ya know, somebody lives here besides you all!"

And she stormed down the corridor like a madwoman just to sneer at me. Soaking wet, nude and hands on both hips, she gyrated her neck, in all directions. The deranged look in her eyes, literally scared the mess out of me. Her dreadlocks flung angrily in the air, as she virtually screamed from the top of her voice. "Where in the hell have you been, anyway? It's three in the morning!"

Perplexed and filled with anxiety, I rushed for the door.

"Where the hell do you think you're going," she stormed. "You can't leave!"

"Hell, if I can't," I said and pushed her away. She hit the wall, slid down, and seizing my thighs, pulled me with her. Without concession, acknowledgment or allowances, I jerked open her knees, clasped her thighs and popped open her legs...

"Is this what you want!" I yelped. "You crazy whore! Are you out of your mind?"

With both hands, I peeled away at her plumpness and clutched her clit with my tongue. She cupped her tiny hardened nipples and panted. "Oh, yes, baby...crazy for you!"

I quickly assessed the situation and decided it was best to get away from this crazy woman when an overwhelming rush came over me. A fierce anticipation set in. The thought of sweeping her off her feet was intriguing, but finally resolving that thought, I fled with a swiftness.

As I drove along Butner Road attempting to sort it out, I realized, short of deep reflection, I was never going to understand Evelyn, nor her near obsession with me. For that matter, I didn't understand any of the housemates who lived with me. But one thing I was sure of, our cozy little foursome had finally ended.

It all happened one Halloween night. It had been a hot day in Atlanta, and the cool October night was welcomed. Whirlpools of bramble brush and pinecones hustled along the narrow, winding roadway as night fell unusually early that evening. With the exception of the moonlit sky vaguely outlining the massive oak and pine trees, not a thing was moving—no cars, no animals, not even children preparing for Halloween festivities. It wouldn't have been unusual to see any number of critters scurrying across the roadway this time of the year. Even deer occasionally lost their way, traveling over the heavily wooded terrain to find themselves at roadside looking confused. But not this night. Not a thing was moving.

I left the ranch about seven o'clock. And as I passed by the entrance, I noticed how madly cluttered it was. Weeping willow trees and massive chunks of weeds blocked the entrance way. The lake was filled with marsh, grown in on all four sides and rounds of hay were strewn everywhere. The land needed bush-hogging badly. Even the horses grazed wearily in the distance. They, too, had been frightfully neglected. I suddenly realized that I hadn't spent much time doing anything lately but swallowing the emptiness that filled me inside.

I'm a news reporter by profession, recently divorced for the second time. Needless to say, I was desperately looking for a lifestyle to replace the one I had grown accustomed to—grasping for something to hold on to and couldn't find. I considered suicide, but decided it wasn't an appropriate option for someone like me with an image to uphold. So, for two years, I struggled with my loneliness and thought of myself as happy sitting at my news desk each morning, typing out stories and spending the remaining hours at home alone. All I had was my work, and even my writing was starting to reflect the pain and sorrow I was feeling.

One morning while sitting at my desk I was surprised with a phone call. The person expressed a genuine tone of excitement and took me back for a moment. It had been a long time since I heard Bishop's voice. I realized, somehow I had lost track of him over the years.

"Well...well...well, if it isn't my long-lost friend Bishop Masters. How the hell are you?"

"Yep! It's me," he said. "I'm just fine...How are you?"

I was instantly reminded of a more pleasant time in my life when I was just starting out as writer, and Bishop was everything I wanted to be as a journalist.

"I'm okay," I responded quietly. "Missed you!"

"Are you still the sexiest woman I know?" he asked.

"Well, maybe I am! But how would you know? You haven't made an attempt to see me."

"That works both ways," he retorted in an even tone.

"Where have you been, anyway, Bishop?"

"Just hanging around..."

"I read your article in *The Daily Times*...had a feeling I knew the writer, turned out it was you. I was happy to know you're still in the loop. You have a distinctive flavor to your work..."

"You like that stuff, huh? Thanks, sweetie! It means a lot to me, coming from you. I've always respected your opinion of my work."

"I'm your biggest fan," I explained, being careful not to sound overly confident or important. I figured Bishop knew I had heard about the television station dropping him last year. After all, the mess he had gotten himself into was all but announced to the world at large. It was all over the news. Being a hermit was the only way you wouldn't have known about it.

"So, you've just been hanging around, huh? Staying out of trouble, Bishop?"

"Yeah, I'm writing a little bit here and there...freelance stuff mostly for the local newspapers... covering specialty stories when somebody wants to pay me to write them."

"How are Lola and the kids?"

"Lola divorced me!"

"Oh! I didn't know that...never know about folks, do you?"

"I guess not. I didn't have a clue. I heard she fell in love with some guy out of Chicago... a big stud type with more time on his hands...or whatever else...know what I mean?"

"Yeah, well...whatcha gonna do now that you're free again?"

"I don't know, sweetie. I'm standing in the question on that...just try to pull it together, I guess. You know...survive!"

Bishop began to tell me more about his marriage breakup, and I told him about mine and that I was in the process of finalizing the decree.

"When did you get married?" he asked.

"A few years ago."

"Damn, I didn't know that...didn't work out, huh?

"Yeah, well... One never knows, does one?"

Bishop laughed. "I know what you mean."

"I've got a great idea, Bishop," I said. "I've got a horse ranch now. Why don't you stay at the ranch? I've got plenty of room. We can work together. What do you think?"

The phone went dead. I'm sure Bishop was wondering what I was getting at with this notion of working together. He admitted he was seeking an alternative means of survival, living with friends and all, and said the suggestion did sound like a perfect opportunity to settle in and pull himself together.

"You live in the boonies, don't you? "I'll need a car out there!"

"Where's your passion for adventure?" I said. "Have you no initiative? Weren't you the one who wrote the article about living in the 'burbs and how lots of people are doing it?"

"Yeah, but I'll still need a car!"

"I have a second car; you can use it. Okay?"

He agreed and moved to the ranch the following week.

Bishop grew to admire the people in the area. They were proud folks, claiming their forty acres and a mule—a piece of land, BMW or Mercedes. They were also folks who understood the meaning of hardship and perseverance. They damn well knew how to survive and were warm and inviting. They touched Bishop in ways he couldn't express. Living at the ranch proved to be a safe haven for a torn man like him.

Sounded like a match made in heaven to me.

Evelyn moved to the ranch two weeks after Bishop. She had recently traveled to Atlanta from the Bahamas and liked it here. She needed to room for a while, she said, and claimed to be looking for a house of her own and that she needed to save some money.

And Conrad, who knows! He moved in shortly after Evelyn.

Soon after we all settled in, I began to engage Bishop in this trumped-up idea I had about developing a think tank, which was a visionary theory at best, he said.

"I want to develop a salon of premium thinkers," I told him with enthusiasm and excitement, nearly animation. While Bishop carefully listened with an open mind, little anticipation and a slight trust in my ability to pull it off, he had his doubts.

"If anyone can do this," he said, "it would probably be you! But there's only one thing. To turn this group into a think tank seems a little far-fetched, doesn't it?"

In retrospect, I would have certainly questioned Evelyn's ability to that end. And you know how the saying goes, Bishop said, laughing, "If somebody wants me on their team...it probably isn't much of a team to begin with!"

And Conrad...who knows?

After long deliberation, Bishop agreed to help me whip this group into something of a think tank, agreeing that the possibilities were limitless if we just gave it a shot.

In the beginning I thought Evelyn and Bishop had just gotten off on the wrong foot. It didn't take a rocket scientist to figure out that the air between them was so thick, you could cut it with a butcher knife. During one of our regularly scheduled think-tank meetings, I got the clear picture that Evelyn disliked Bishop more than I realized. She said something about how he was a good reporter, but he wasn't refined!

"Me, not refined?" Bishop huffed, naturally resenting the comment. She didn't even know him, he said. And being the quintessential media man that he considered himself, I imagine Bishop couldn't understand where she got the unmitigated gall to address him in that way. And he let her know in no uncertain terms...

"You know absolutely nothing about me," he cracked. "You've got a lot of nerve. Who the hell do you think you are, anyway? Just because your father's a lawyer. So what? What do you know about being re-fined, absolutely zip!"

"Well...you're not refined," Evelyn quietly retorted.

"You say any old thing that pops into your head and..."

"Okay! Can we please continue?" I said, raising my hand.

Reluctantly, they agreed, but eyed each other during the entire session.

Evelyn was thirty-two and had never married. You might have guessed why, had you seen her up close and personal. She did sort of look like a dried-up frog with huge horn-rimmed glasses. She was Twiggy thin, too, and ghostly pale! And she had a real personality problem, like she had permanent PMS or something.

Like I said...shortly after she moved in, she started in on Bishop's case.

"Bishop do this...Bishop do that," assuming a role of more than just a housemate—a housewife was more like it!

"You all act like savages," she said. "No class whatsoever!"

Evelyn became more and more irritating as time went on. But we learned to tolerate her for the sake of our agreed union. Actually, we felt sorry for her. All she seemed to do was stay cooped up in her room all night by herself, doing God only knows what!

Bishop had his ways, too. He claimed I was a would-be writer, the kind who is always writing several novels at the same time and never finishing any of them.

"Actually, you're potentially a pretty good writer," he told me one day. "But finish something, why don't you? Finish something, creative asshole!"

I have a huge library of books, ranging from steamy love novels to intense war-strategy books. I didn't necessarily like sharing them unless one was serious about expanding his horizons.

One day, Evelyn wanted to expand her mind, she said, and asked if she could take several books from the library to read. Later in the week, I wanted to know how she was enjoying them, so I asked her how the reading was coming.

"Good stories," she replied. And that was it!

She probably didn't read a thing. Actually, I think she just wanted to know what I knew and figured that if she read my books, the knowledge would transcend miraculously into some kind of insight into what made me tick.

"That's a joke, too!" Bishop said, because I never finished anything I read either!

I wondered if Bishop had a hidden psychological problem with that

58

habit of his. He was always shifting blame. Quiet as it's kept, he was the one who never finished anything he read or wrote. Of course, being the more disciplined writer in the house, I was encouraging him. He claimed to be doing the same thing with me.

Sometimes, we felt compassionate toward Evelyn. Well, we tried to be considerate, let's put it that way. Actually, we felt sorry for her, because she never seemed to do anything but read, complain and spend all night cooped up in her room. But not this particular night. This night, she found it necessary to come out of her den to harass us.

Bishop and I had been at Grant Park all day, covering the Juneteenth celebration, sponsored by the Jomandi Theater. I was meeting some friends I hadn't seen in years. We were both pumped up with excitement.

"I want to write something favorable about this event," Bishop said. "I'm sure I'll be comfortable in that kind of musical environment and all, but it isn't necessarily my element, it's yours. I'm a newsman...know what I mean?"

"Yeah, I do," I replied. "And some of my close friends are performing. I can get us backstage!"

"Hey! Wait a minute," Bishop said, annoyed. "I have a press pass. After all, I am a news reporter. I don't need you to get me backstage. I just want you to go because you have that element of charisma everybody likes."

There was a moment of silence between us.

I might have been a little condescending here, I admit. Bishop did look at me with a smirk on his face, not knowing how I took the left-field compliment he threw at me. I'm sure he figured I knew he was massaging my ego, anyway. So I let it go at that with nothing more to say but, "Yeah, yeah, Bishop...I do captivate people, and I do look better than you!"

"Ya know, princess!" he replied.

Hatchets buried, we went to the function together.

The next day, Bishop sat in his cubicle in the newsroom typing out the story and was overwhelmed by a gush of endorphins.

He set the layout to read: *While the pundits, politicians and pretty people gushed about the opening of Planet Hollywood, an estimated 50,000*

*African-Americans partied in Grant Park. Kudos to Jomandi Theater, for
staging a monstrous, albeit marvelous Juneteenth festival, featuring acts like
the BarKays, Cool Joe and Mystique. Not only did the music make for a
mellow mood, but the spirit of the celebration gave it a distinctive flavor
and vibe...*

"You like that pretty stuff, don't you?" he said. "But what I was
really thinking about when I penned that pretty prose was what it might
be like to screw the crap out of Evelyn and listen to her scream while I
did it! On second thought," he said, "I wouldn't screw her with your
dog!"

I did wonder whether screwing her real good might make the difference in that irritable personality of hers but concluded Bishop wasn't
the one.

Or was I? Hmmm...

Like I said, this particular Saturday night about eleven o'clock,
Bishop and I had just gotten in from the Grant Park celebration, preparing to go back out when Evelyn stormed down the hall and howled at
us. Perhaps it had been my fault that Evelyn was treating us all like children and had taken over our lives the way she had. I gave Evelyn the
title The Wife one day when she took it upon herself to put a chores
agenda together for all the housemates and politely announced that
there would be a house meeting every Sunday.

"All of you are to make sure that the chores I've assigned you are
carried out," she asserted. Then demanded that everyone show up at the
house meeting on Sunday—"or else!"

Or else? Or else, what?

No one really wanted to know.

The Wife did indeed describe her behavior but I think Evelyn took
it too far. She was even proud of it. It seemed funny to us when we
teased her about the title, laughingly for the most part, but she would
get really pissed. Although Evelyn certainly acted like a wife to us all,
she was decidedly different with the men than with me. For me, she
would shop, clean, wash my clothes and cut my hair, but refused to do
anything like that for the men. In fact, she went out of her way to make
them uncomfortable, and believe me, they were.

"No comment," Conrad said one day when Bishop mentioned to

60

him about how Evelyn was treating us all like children. Bishop was looking for support on this one—confirmation of his thinking about this woman. "But all I got from this asshole," he told me, "was gotta go, Bishop!"

I did overhear Conrad tell Bishop later that day, "That Evelyn's a mess. She never gives up," after an encounter with her about mowing the back lawn.

Sitting in the den with me was what Evelyn seemed to enjoy most. One day, while sitting in the den together, Evelyn uttered a surprisingly suggestive statement. "Wouldn't it be nice if we lived here together...just the two of us, without the men?" she asked. "I like you—a lot!" I might have agreed under different circumstances, except the thought of being alone in the house with just Evelyn would have been maddening, to say the least, ghastly, even grueling!

Shortly after that day, Evelyn put another chores agenda together. This time she wrote it on the dry-erase board, located by the front door. She claimed nobody listened to her, which is why she chose this method. It was curious that it only included the men.

In bold letters the board read:

SATURDAY 5/20

BISHOP...MOW FRONT LAWN, BRUSH AND FEED HORSES

CONRAD...MOW THE BACK LAWN, LUNGE AND LET HORSES OUT TO GRAZE

In bolder letters:

'CAUSE YOU LAZY SON OF A BITCHES SLEEP ALL DAY!!!!

The next morning, Evelyn got up early to execute her plan, making sure the men followed through with her instructions. Naturally, she woke up Bishop first!

Bishop had been out all night working on a piece about strip clubs. He said he needed to do some research, requiring him to cover the clubs around town and interview the tabletop dancers up close and personal. Bishop had just gotten in bed with Monica on his mind, one of the tabletop dancers, he interviewed that night, and was caught in a very precarious position.

"I was in the process of falling asleep with a big beautiful hard-on," he told me, "and I heard this screeching voice...'come on Bishop, get up!'

"It was Evelyn howling through the crack of my bedroom door. She flung open the door and screamed at the top of her voice...'the lawn looks like a field of corn!' she howled.

"The cry of her voice sounded like it came from the planet Mars. It was unbearable! I don't give a good goddamn what the frickin' lawn looks like," I told her. Okay!

"I pretended to be awake, holding the newspaper in front of my face, like I was reading.

"'You witch! I mumbled. You irritate the shit out of me!'

"I mean, I held the paper up in front of my face, until hell could have frozen over.

"And she was still there!"

As Bishop told me the story, I personally never figured out how she caught him with that stunt. The newspaper up in front of his face ploy had always worked on his wife, he said. "In fact, when she would come in the room some mornings to wake me for work, it gave me at least twenty more minutes to close my eyes."

It had always worked with me, too, and everybody else, for that matter. But not with this woman. She was relentless! Evelyn wouldn't give up either. She kept coming back until Bishop eventually got out of bed with him attempting to deck her. She ran out of the room crying. Bishop mumbled to himself, hoping she would overhear him...

"I swear...I'm gonna nail that nut one of these days—while she's sleeping preferably. And then before she knows it...*bam*...too late! She would have already died from multiple orgasms. Her last screech on my behalf."

Disgruntled, Bishop handled his chores.

Conrad was not as willing a subject as Bishop, especially so early on a Saturday morning. His limousine service had him on twenty-four-hour call, he claimed. He was always going on an important pickup, or just coming back from one. Evelyn quietly asked him to get out of bed and handle his chores. I think she talked to him softly because she wasn't sure what his reaction to her demands would be. He wasn't around all that much and didn't talk a whole lot either, so there was no telling.

"I'm a very busy man," he would respond. "I'll get to it...soon as I can!"

Which he never did...Kudos to Conrad!

By the way, none of the housemates understood Conrad. He was different, secretive and never seemed to have any time for anyone but himself. He was self-centered and didn't contribute to anything around the house, not even a lousy conversation. We all had our doubts about Conrad, anyway. We weren't quite sure of who he was, or what he was, for that matter. Guessing was all anyone could do about Conrad. Attempting a conversation with him would inevitably begin and end with, "Don't have time to talk, gotta go!"

Conrad didn't have his own room. He slept with Evelyn. Nobody understood that either. No one, except maybe Evelyn, and she claimed they weren't engaged in an intimate relationship. They were just room-mates, she said. It was a platonic relationship.

Platonic during the day!

At first, none of the housemates believed that Evelyn and Conrad weren't having hot, steamy sex at night, since Conrad came home very early in the morning, usually around four o'clock. Bishop told me that he would be listening for Conrad to open the bedroom door around that time, and secretly wished he wouldn't show up and just maybe, Evelyn would let him come in the room instead.

If you looked at Evelyn real good, she did sort of look like she was wearing a turtleneck, kind of backed up. "I'd be willing to help her with that," Bishop suggested one day.

"...Straighten her right out!"

Conrad did stay out all night on occasion. What he did at night became a constant item of discussion with Evelyn. "What do you think Conrad does when he's out all night? Why won't he make love to me?"

After the umpteenth time, Bishop was fed up.

"I don't give a flying gnat's ass what he does! Get rid of the son of a bitch. I'll screw you and be glad to do it!"

Evelyn didn't appreciate that. In fact, she lashed back. "Bishop, why don't you drop dead. I want an apology from you, right now!"

Bishop didn't apologize.

"Why don't you shut the hell up then about this asshole. I'm sick of you," he said, and stormed off, mumbling.

There was some truth in what he said. She did talk to anyone who would listen, about this situation comedy of hers with Conrad. It had gotten to the point where inevitably, she would start all of her conversations with "My sleeping partner never tries anything with me..."

My god, I was sick of it, too!

"I know what's wrong with him," Bishop explained to her one day. "He's too tired to do anything with you after he gets done screwin' all his other whores. A guy can handle but so much, and look at you. Who in his right mind would want to screw you, anyway?"

Bishop's girlfriend suggested one day that Evelyn should hire a private investigator to follow Conrad one night and find out something about him, anything, and end this obsession of hers with him, once and for all. I thought it was a good idea, so I relayed the suggestion to Evelyn. She seemed intrigued by the idea, but instead, rushed out and bought this book called *The Invisible Life*, written by a female author who described a woman going through a similar experience. She claimed the book might help her in supporting this theory she had about men who never consummate their relationships, and had an outside life, separate and secretive. I don't think Evelyn found out the author's explanation. She never got past the first chapter. The bookmark indicated that all she was doing was carrying the book around with her, like a reference manual or something. Frankly, I don't think she really wanted to know!

Sometimes, Conrad would be gone for days at a time. It did seem curious to us that Evelyn would have other men in her bedroom at night, and never seemed to worry about Conrad showing up. So, we figured she and Conrad must have a kind of special relationship—an alternative lifestyle—we just didn't understand. We finally believed their relationship was platonic and stopped canvassing the hallway at night, corralled to listen for hollers and screams expected to spiral from their bedroom door. We decided that if Conrad ever changed his mind, we would be the first to know. Evelyn would surely tell.

Like I said, Saturday night looked promising for both Bishop and me, until Evelyn started in on my case with this gibberish. "You promised we were going to the Sports Bar tonight...just the two of us...you forgot already?" she said and walked toward me with her arms extended. "You promised!"

64

My mouth flew open, and we all stopped. All focus was on Evelyn. Conrad raced toward the door, carrying a little ragged blue travel bag he had always been careful not to let out of his sight. Bishop was writing his weekly news column that was already past deadline. And I was toying with a brilliant angle for a story on sexual fantasies. All minds went completely blank from Evelyn's disruption.

"Why don't you shut the hell up, Evelyn!" Bishop scowled. "Who in the hell cares what you're doing? Can't you see I'm working? I can't hear myself think!"

"Thinking was your first mistake, Bishop!" Evelyn howled, turning up her nose and sauntering down the hall. She looked back at me and pointed. "You promised... just the two of us!"

I quickly interrupted her, blew a kiss in her direction, circumventing the anticipated ranting and raving, and in a fluster she retreated to her room.

Thank God!

Bishop started mocking Evelyn. "You promised... just the two of us," he teased. "The Wife is talking to you...She wuvs you...She wants you!"

"She secretly wants you—not me!" I said, and laughed.

At the time it didn't register with me how Evelyn really felt, certainly not the way the others saw it. But then it did become more clear when Evelyn came into my room nude one night after taking a shower. She asked if she could borrow some lotion.

I handed her the lotion. "Would you...?" she asked, and climbed on my bed and sprawled.

My bed is four feet off the ground, a pretty tall order for tiny Evelyn, who looked like she was being served up as she lay across it. Her pubic mound protruded against the thinness of her body, and like a baby's butt, her pubic area was completely shaved clean. Her tiny clit peeked out from behind her loose folds and stood straight up. When I began to smooth the lotion over her breasts, her legs eased open and her almond-shaped nipples hardened.

She began to shiver.

"Oooooh...baby, your hands are ice cold!" she exclaimed, laying otherwise motionless, except for the light twitching of her body. She watched me freely as I pumped lotion in the palms of my hands and rub them together vigorously. When I touched her, she involuntarily began to shake. I calmed her, covering her body with wide sweeps across her shoulders, then down along the sides of her body and along the flat of her stomach. When I reached her pelvic area, I cupped my hands around her groin then lifted her up and massaged her clit. Her legs fell open immediately.

"Oooooh, that's good, baby," she moaned. "More...I'm lovin' it!"

Evelyn began to pant as if out of breath and grabbed my face, pressing it between her legs. "Do me, baby," she begged. "Do me!"

"What the hell's goin' on in there," I heard Bishop shout. "What are you all doing?"

I wondered where that scene might have taken me had Bishop not interrupted. I left Evelyn dazzled with anticipation.

Like I said, this particular Saturday night about eleven o'clock, Bishop and I had just gotten in from the Grant Park celebration and were preparing to go back out that evening, when Evelyn reminded me of our plans to go to the Sports Bar...

"Wife," I explained, "my plans have changed! But you can go with Bishop and me to the new jazz club downtown. Want to go...?"

"I don't want to go with you and Bishop anywhere," Evelyn responded and stormed off to her room in a huff. The truth was I didn't want to go anywhere with Evelyn. The last time we went out, she literally showed her ass—mooned me in the parking lot at a Fish Bones' restaurant when I informed her I was late for a meeting and had to leave.

"I'll see you tonight at the club," Bishop finally said, leaving alone. "If The Wife lets you, come out tonight!"

I sighed with great trepidation. "You're leaving me with her?" I asked. "Some friend you are!"

Deep down, I knew Bishop had done the right thing. Had we left together, this woman would have called out the militia on his ass, or dialed 911 and had him arrested for theft by taking.

Bishop sat at the bar listening to Francois, a friend he hadn't seen in years tell him about his stay in Europe. "I was forced out of the country, man," he explained. "I got all messed up!"

Bishop understood Francois' dilemma but was wondering where he had gotten the name Francois. Since last he remembered, this joker's name was Frank or something like that, he said. Francois continued to explain his saga, and Bishop listened with boredom written all over his face, yawning throughout.

"The conspiracy mess I got myself into caused me to move out of the country for three years, man," Francois explained. "The industry blackballed my ass...."

"That's rough!" Bishop commented, wondering if Francois thought that moving out of the country made him seem important.

"Got in a little mess myself some time back," Bishop retorted.

"Got out of it though...used my contacts with the boys in the media."

Francois never got to finish his story nor did Bishop. Their attention was redirected to the front entrance of the bar. Evelyn and I entered hand-in-hand.

I noticed Francois first. He was looking lustily at us.

"Wonder who that is?" I said to Evelyn.

Evelyn didn't respond but spotted Bishop and immediately put her arm around my waist as if she was staking a property claim. I didn't pay much attention to it. I was focused on Francois.

Bishop introduced me to Francois. Francois smiled, looking like he came on himself with a stupid shit-eating grin on his face, showing all thirty-twos.

"Hello!" Francois said with an obviously deepened voice.

I smiled as he leaned in, gave me a kiss and whispered in my ear. "Are you the beautiful one? Bishop told me about you. Will you be spending the evening with us?"

He's pretty aggressive, I thought, and before I could respond, Bishop leaned in and whispered in my ear. "Francois might make a good housemate. He's an actor...very creative...you'll like him."

Incidently, Bishop didn't mean one word of that crap. The last thing he wanted was male competition. I introduced Evelyn to Francois, and Evelyn waved at him with a sort of brushed-off gesture. It seemed to her that Francois was more interesting for the moment than she was, which wasn't all that hard to begin with, and gave me a good deal of satisfaction. Evelyn seemed intimidated by Francois' deep baritone voice and knew right away I was interested in him. Formalities concluded, Francois and Bishop asked us to join them at a table, and Evelyn responded by screwing up her face.

Francois confronted Evelyn with a real deep, sexy voice..."Is there a problem?" he said, and looked her directly in the eyes.

Evelyn stormed off, shrugging her shoulders. Minutes later, she grabbed some poor guy who looked about eighteen, holding on to his private parts like they were a treasure of jewels. They hovered together in the corner,

playing touchy-feely games and whispering. I continued to sit at the bar with Francois and Bishop, watching this charade, when Bishop's date, Joanne, walked in.

Francois and I decided to check out this new club called Ying Yang on Spring Street and asked Bishop and Joanne to join us. "Do you all wanna come?" I asked.

"Yeah...Why not?" Bishop said. "I could use a change of pace right about now. I've been waiting for Joanne for more than an hour!"

I winked at Joanne as she offered Bishop an explanation for her tardiness...

"Sorry, sweetie" she purred. "I was dressing extra pretty for you." She stuck her finger in her mouth, licked her heavily painted lips and cooled Bishop right out.

"It's all good," Francois added, putting his arm around my waist. The four of us left the bar.

Bishop gathered I was thinking about Evelyn's behavior—grabbing the first guy she saw and carrying him off the way she did.

"You look pensive," he said. "That Evelyn's a whore, isn't she?"

"Yeah, well...I guess. She must be something like that!" I said.

The club was crowded with people packed inside like sardines and standing around outside like vultures canvassing for carcasses. It reminded me of a jazz spot straight out of Greenwich Village—sawdust on the floor, no air conditioning, serving only wine and beer. The band was blasting one of Jimi Hendrix's cuts "Crosstown Traffic."

Francois turned to me with a gleam in his eye. "They know me here. We won't have to pay."

He looked at Bishop in a rather curtly manner.

"So frickin' what," Bishop whispered in my ear. "If he's so damn important, how is it I never saw him on television, or in a performance with any consequence, except that sitcom I don't remember the name of...playing a cop or something...a walk-on part with three words to say, 'Raise your hands!' Big deal!"

I raised my finger to my lips to quiet Bishop while Francois ordered drinks.

Bishop scanned the club for a possible news story, periodically focusing on Francois' moves. Francois handed me a drink and then sat close. Bishop gave me a sorrowful puppy-dog look when Francois escorted me to the dance floor on the other side of the club. I realized that Bishop must have made a fatal mistake, an error in judgment, because the way he was watching us, I don't think he meant for us to like each other so much.

Francois rested both of his arms on my shoulders and nuzzled his nose in the nap of my neck as we danced. He began kissing my forehead, my neck, then between my breasts. He suddenly gabbed a nipple with his tongue and sweetly nibbled. Butterflies began fluttering. I could feel the bulge in his pants protruding against my leg. I secretly swept my hand across it then palmed it. We left the club together, holding hands.

"Not a word from either of them," Bishop complained to Joanne. "No good-bye...no thanks...kiss my ass...or anything!"

Despite his avid vow to remain unattached to me, Bishop was grief-stricken. Later Joanne told me that his real concern was my safety, since he knew something about Francois' prowess. He told me that he was canvassing the thought of Francois and me making love in Francois' penthouse and wished it was him instead. Joanne became irritated by Bishop's distraction and poked him in the ribs, licked her lips and smiled. Bishop was cool.

Francois' penthouse was luxurious—a huge tri-level, white carpeted and heavily mirrored setting. Mirrors were everywhere, even on his bedroom ceiling. Right away, he stripped naked, then walked over to the bar. He looked back at me. "What's your pleasure!" he whispered in a deep, sultry voice.

I was much too busy looking over his eight-pack to answer him right away. His stomach muscles were mounded beautifully descending into eight evenly separated tiers, and curved smoothly into his chocolate swank that swung like a horse. I was drawn—immediately. I leaned against his buns and wrapped my hands around his waist, feeling his hefty protrusion.

When he turned around, I looked deep in his eyes. "Absolute... vodka, martini, "I whispered and slid my hand along the shaft of his hardness and comfortably fondled him.

"...Olive or twist?" he asked.

I squatted, slipped him in my mouth and mumbled...

"Olives...lots of olives!"

"Now, or later?" he asked.

"Now, and later!" I replied and licked his length.

He slowly began moving himself back and forth, moaning and handling the maneuver gently in and out of my mouth.

He pulled me up...

"Absolute...vodka, martini...with lots of olives!" he whispered and handed me the drink. The mirrored bar reflected his tight-end buns as I drank. He began to strip me naked, fondling my skin along the way. He knew what he was doing alright. No question about his prowess. When I was completely nude, he stood and looked at me, as if examining a purchase.

He twirled me around. "Damn...you're fine!" he said. "Thick!"

I leaned against him, and he began massaging my neck and shoulders and along the sides of my arms. He reached over my shoulders and swept his hands across my breasts, squeezed them gently then cupped them.

"Your skin is so smooth," he said and swept his hands down along my spine. His eyes followed every move he made. He smoothed out my back as I perked up and locked my legs for the perfect fit. He slid himself slowly, evenly and smoothly inside me, feeling my walls along the way. "Ohhhhh," I moaned. "Ooooooh! Stretch, baby, stretch!" I said.

He reached for my breasts, pulled me to him and sat down with me in his lap. Straddling his thick thighs, he eased my body down. I slid down his shaft like a key into a lock, pacified and calmed. His soothing glide increased my tranquility, reaching and searching for the bottom.

He fondled my breasts, kissed and cuddled me way down deep, forcing his surge deeper and deeper inside me. He wriggled his loins with each stroke. He reached the far corners of my sanity as I panted, and my upper torso surged forward. He swiveled me to one side and stood me up, lifted my leg to meet his and thrust himself deep inside me. He gripped the top of my thigh and held it close to his body. I could feel the tingle of tiny fine hairs stand on his arms as he moved my thigh back and forth and plunged.

"I like it, baby!" he said. "Oh yeah, I like it...Open it all the way up for me, baby!"

I opened wider and squatted slightly so he could reach deeper.

"Uhhhhh...Oooooh...Oh, yeah, baby. Oh! Yes, baby. Oooooo!" I huffed and cried. He sucked air and blew out, snorted and growled.

"You good-pussy witch! Ooooooh, you sweet whore!" he wailed. "Give...it...to...me!"

An explosion went off in my head. Cream of cum flowed through my veins right to the soft spot on top of my head.

"Ooooow...Oooooooh," I howled, and tears flowed from my eyes. Juices ripped from my body, and sweat poured from all over me. I collapsed with pacification that landed me right on the floor. I couldn't move. He picked me up and placed me on the sofa face up. He spread my legs, clamping them down on either side in a frog like position and popped himself in. The sloshing and charging was eager as he gyrated in and out with ease.

An explosion contorted his face. "Ooooooh, girl...Oh, girl!" he howled. "Martini?" he asked, exhausted.

"Oh, yes," I replied, with instant replay in mind.

I left Francois that night, passed out on the floor. When I arrived back at the ranch, both Bishop and his girl were pissy drunk. They were hollering at the top of their voices, falling all over each other, giggling.

Conrad had arrived just before I did and was sitting in the den.

"Did you move somebody else in?" Conrad asked. "There's a strange car in my parking space, a Lexus or something."

"No!" I responded. "I think that car belongs to that guy!" I said, pointing to the guy following Evelyn, coming down the corridor. Evelyn's hair was all over her head. Her lipstick was frightfully smeared around her mouth, and she was being trailed by the young boy she retrieved from the club earlier that night.

"Everybody, this is Larry," she announced, then sneered at me.

Larry grinned, exposing little crab like teeth, said nothing and continued trailing Evelyn out of the door.

"What was that?" Conrad asked, as if he were interested.

"A problem, I think...of a personal nature!" I responded.

Conrad got up, excused himself by bowing his head, went to his room and slammed the door behind him.

"What happened with you and Francois?" Joanne asked, running into the den with Bishop trailing behind her. Joanne covered her mouth as if to stop herself from talking and giggled.

"That Francois is something else," I said. "For two hours he performed what seemed like the entire script from the play *Othello*. I couldn't believe it! Don't get me wrong. He did have a wholesome, entertaining baritone voice but then when he began the dialogue from *Macbeth*, it was a bit much. What an ego!"

"The juicy stuff please," Yvonne said, giggling.

"Oh...Yeah, sorry...Ummm, anyway..."

"Well...what did you all do after you left the club?" she asked.

"Not much!" I lied. "At that point, I was thinking of how to get the heck away from him. After we got in the car, he began to interrogate me...

"What is it you want from your life?" he asked.

"I told him sarcastically, mostly to be left alone!

"Then he asked, 'What do you want from me?'

"I told him again, to be left alone and turned the radio up loud to get my point across. He turned the radio down...I ignored him and turned the radio up higher. All of a sudden he told me to pull the car over. I did. He jumped out and raised his hands over his head, like he was going to stretch or something and grabbed his head. I could see him shaking his hands toward heaven like a madman in my rearview mirror.

"Get out!" he shouted.

"I pulled off! All I know is, I was rid of him!"

Bored, Bishop started unbuttoning his girlfriend's blouse. I watched Joanne's torpedo tits jump out as Bishop grabbed her raspberry-perked nipples and covered them with furious suckling noises. He looked at me, grinned, licked his lips and shoved his hand up her dress.

A loud bang then a crunch surfaced from the garage. Bishop jumped up, Joanne lightly pulled her blouse together, and we all showed up at the garage at the same time. Together we flung the door open. I don't know about the other housemates but my guess is they thought the same thing I did. My idea about Evelyn was confirmed. She had serious problems and no doubt was not in control of her faculties. Evelyn was completely nude, kneeling on the hood of the little crab-tooth boy's car. He was behind her, humping away. It appeared that they had just fallen off the roof of the car in heated passion and landed on the hood.

Rain and thunder lit up the sky.

"My god!" I said. "What will the neighbors think!"

Bishop and Joanne just stood with their mouths open.

Evelyn saw us and dashed into the house, leaving the boy behind. Buck naked, drenching wet and looking deranged, she ran straight into her bedroom and slammed the door behind her. Larry threw his clothes in the car and took off, racing down the driveway, sliding and skidding in madness.

We rushed straight to Evelyn's bedroom door, turned the knob. It was locked. All ears were glued. We heard the voices of Evelyn and Conrad...

Evelyn was crying, and Conrad was asking her what was the matter. The picture of her thin, nude body popped in my head as it probably did all of us. We gazed at one another and covered our mouths, snickering in anticipation.

Then we heard...

"You're doing something here tonight, stud!" Evelyn shouted in a drunken stupor. "You're full of it, Conrad," she bellowed. "Get over here!"

"Go away!" Conrad said, calmly but annoyed.

Evelyn began to scream... "You're an asshole, Conrad...You must be a faggot or something!" and stormed out of the room.

Draped in a short, bright red, see-all-the-way through negligee, Evelyn held an assortment of belts in each hand. She was on a mission. She held the belts up high for us to see, winked and said with a deter-

73

mined look in her eyes, "I'm going to tie this asshole down, and we'll see what he does then!"

We looked at one another and began laughing.

"Has the girl lost her mind?" Joanne asked.

We didn't really know what to think at this point. Evelyn had displayed restraint and calmness in these matters, as far as we knew. She was irritable on occasion, but plainly thought of as conservative.

Bishop laughed and said, "Refined...If you know what I mean!"

We followed Evelyn down the corridor, engaged in egging her on...

"Do it...Do it...Evelyn...Yeah! Do it!" we all chimed. "Go for it! Let's find out if he's a real man, or what!"

Joanne enticed her, ran to the den and poured three huge water glasses, filled to the brim, with rich, dark Southern Comfort.

...And the charade was on!

Evelyn smiled back at us when she turned the bedroom doorknob.

"It's locked!" she said and looked back at us again, ran her tongue over her red-painted lips, bit her bottom lip, then entered the room through the adjoining bathroom.

Conrad was in the shower.

We listened from the hallway in anticipation, falling all over one another, trying to get a full account of what was about to happen. Then all of a sudden, Evelyn swung open the door and ran out shouting at the top of her voice "He's hung...he's hung...he's hung!" she screamed.

Well, I don't need to tell you, we knew this woman needed help. We looked at one another flabbergasted, I assure you. Evelyn had totally lost it! She suddenly grabbed my hand, causing me to spill my drink all over myself and dragged me into the bathroom. Conrad shot by us, jolting like a flash of lightning. He was nude, his private parts swinging on either side of his thighs, headed toward the kitchen. Evelyn ran through the den, heading him off at the pass, and when Conrad arrived in the kitchen, Evelyn was draped over the kitchen table in her bright red dolly, with lips to match. She snapped open the snatch bottom of her dolly and smiled.

"Look at that!" Bishop bellowed, running into the room and licking his lips.

"Oooooh, yeah! That thing is everywhere," Conrad howled. "Whoa!"

Conrad ran over to her as if mesmerized by what he saw and slipped himself right in. He jabbed into her opened exposure with several, rough movements, then like a slow vibrator, oozed himself in and out, and took off again. Evelyn met him head-on around the corner. She bent over again, opened layers of sweetness with her hands, all up in his face...

"Come on, slip that thing in here," she beckoned and pulled up her dolly snatch again, ripping it away from her body. Conrad stepped all in it this time, humped over like a dog in heat. By the time we all gathered, Conrad was giving Evelyn the shakes. She was screaming and cumming for her life. She was out of control and hollering at the top of her voice..."Gimme that...gimme all that..." she said. "I knew you had it in you. Now I got it in me!"

Evelyn dropped to her knees, swung around and threw him deep-throat in her mouth. She churned and sucked as he swelled in her mouth. She came up for air only seconds, then shoved him back in again, like she was in a sucking contest, chewing and nibbling profusely. She grabbed his bulbous balls and fondled them wildly, grabbing and clasping in the heat of passion as she slurped and sucked.

Bishop and I looked at each other in disbelief.

Conrad looked up at me. "What about you? You want some, too?" he asked.

While still on her knees, Evelyn grabbed my hand and pulled me to her. She ripped off the top of my dress and started sucking my nipples, grabbing at my pubic area and feeling for my opening. She grabbed and yanked and raked her fingers all in me, squeezed and gyrated her fingers inside, then up and down, until I was sopping wet. She grabbed Conrad's pulsating rivulet, pulled him down to the floor and shoved it in me. He was hot, thick and rock hard.

"Damn!" Bishop shouted to Conrad. "What's up with this? Don't you see me here? Don't you need some help? You can't handle this by yourself!"

"I got it, Bishop!" Conrad assured him, stroking me while Evelyn nibbled and sucked my pointed, hard nipples, and Bishop looked on.

Evelyn jerked Conrad out of me, pushed me on the floor and pinned my legs in back of my head. She knelt down and began slurping. Conrad ran around Evelyn and took advantage of her perked rear end and entered her with very slow gyrations.

"My god!" she screamed. "This is heaven sent!"

"Damn!" Bishop said. "Yeah, something's up with this guy...selfish mutha..."

Bishop's girlfriend ran out of the room, dashed to her car, and Bishop followed her racing down the driveway.

Then like something from the *Legend of Sleepy Hollow,* the sky turned black. A tornado like whirlpool of lightning streaks and roaring thunder lit up the sky. It was like God Himself was speaking to us. Evelyn got overly excited and stood, shoving her body against mine, then hugged me tightly as if scared to death. I grabbed her and began spanking her bottom.

"Ooooh, baby...Yessssss!" she screamed. "That's what I want and grabbed me around the waist. She fell down, and her legs flew up as I began massaging between her legs with every other blow to her bottom.

"You look like you know what you're doing," Conrad interjected, curiously.

"You want some?" I asked.

"Yeah, I want some of that snatch of yours," he confessed, and knelt behind me and shoved all nine inches up in me. I screamed and cooed like a bird.

I was leaning over Evelyn when I saw Bishop coming down the corridor. I pushed back onto Conrad's movement. It was feeling real good to me. So, I leaned farther back on him and with one sharp snap, ripped Evelyn's frayed negligee totally off.

Bishop's eyes widened as he came closer.

"What in the hell is going on here?" he asked.

No one paid attention to Bishop or what he was saying, explosions blew off in everybody's head. The smell of sex was everywhere.

"I want to maybe even be invited to join," Bishop said. "Know what I mean?"

Conrad pulled himself out of me after the explosion in his head dizzied him to the point of swaggering. I got up, lightly smacked Evelyn on her bottom and nodded for her to follow me.

Conrad and Bishop stood there watching, amazed. Evelyn and I looked back at them smiling provocatively like two Cheshire cats who just caught Tweety Bird. Then like a whisper of warm air that comes and goes, we vanished into my bedroom.

"Not a word," Bishop said to Conrad. "Not even a false explanation!"

"Gotta go...Bishop," Conrad replied. "Don't have time to talk!"

Our cozy little foursome was over. Now it would be a nice, neat twosome—Evelyn and me.

Dolores Bundy

The Forbidden

Art of Desire

by
Cole Riley

THE EX FILES

It was one of the worst winters the city had ever endured. More than five feet of snow fell in less than a day, and more was to come. Many businesses were closed, classes canceled and all but the most essential city services were on a forced holiday. Joanne didn't have to go to her job as a linguist at a private school in midtown, because many of the roads into work were completely covered with snowdrifts, concealing a thick sheet of treacherous ice underneath. That was not the case with her husband, Wayne, the head of publicity department for a Wall Street firm. His wife couldn't understand why he didn't just call the company and say he couldn't make it due to the nasty weather.

"I can't do that because I've got to finish the paperwork on the Seraphim account," Wayne said, taking off his pajama top and glancing again at the alarm clock.

"If I don't go in, the work won't get done, and that's almost four million dollars in business right down the drain. Gotta go in."

"Can't somebody else go in for you?" she asked, trying to find another way to keep him home. "There must be somebody closer to the city that could go in. I don't understand why every time there's some kind of crisis, everything always falls on you. They don't pay you enough for this kind of loyalty."

"Joanne, it must be done," he said, going into the bathroom. "Could you fix me a cup of coffee, please, sweet?"

81

Irked by his dedication to a job that didn't pay him nearly enough for him to go out into a blizzard, Joanne walked to the bathroom door and stood, watching him wash up in the sink. If he was going to race out into the cold, he'd forego his morning shower so he could make the eight-ten train into Penn Station. Why was he so eager to go to work? Maybe he couldn't stand being with her anymore. Maybe it was something else. Maybe it was his new, pretty young secretary. She'd spoken to the wench on the phone and didn't like her easy, casual manner. The woman was too friendly for her good. How was she with him? Maybe there was something going on with the two of them. He seemed to work late a lot lately and when he got home, he was usually too tired to do anything. In so many ways, she was bored to death with marriage, family and routine.

But it wasn't always like that. During their first year of dating, she told Wayne that she loved him as much as she could. Maybe it would deepen as time went by. He never really understood what she meant. In those days, she had one man after another. She built a reputation for making men suffer, but it didn't chase him away. He wanted her more. Back then, she got off sexually on exhibitionism and anything else weird, nothing but those kinky things made her excited about living or loving. A rebellion against her strict upbringing in a military household. It was her mission to unleash the freak in Wayne, to loosen him up. Their dates became a series of wild parties, private spots with over-the-top activities and underground sex shows.

One Friday night, she took Wayne to an underground frolic club in the Bronx with a heavy Latino and black crowd, and the party was hopping when they arrived. She could see things were heating up through the haze of thick cigarette smoke and the overhead spinning colored lights, girls writhing to the hot tropical beat almost naked with their breasts exposed and jeans open and guys grinding against them with their pants unzipped and dicks out. It was an anything-goes atmosphere, no limits, no rules. The longer the party lasted, the more uninhibited the night became. She'd always wanted to seduce and screw a man in front of an audience, to ravish him and work everybody watching into a sexual frenzy. Lots of people watching her getting hot and heavy with a man, the center of attention. This was the night for it.

With a smoldering Machito tune with a Cuban clave beat cooking in the background, she ripped open Wayne's shirt, popping the buttons and started sucking his nipples. Drunk on rum, he closed his eyes and let her have her way. She wanted to hurt him with desire. She pressed her lips to his chest, tasting his male scent of sweat and cologne, listening to him softly murmur his joy of having her in his life.

A wave of gasps and sighs went through the crowd when she kneeled and undid his pants, removing his dick. Completely hard, sticking straight up. She wondered what it would be like to be a man with a throbbing erection like his, about to pop. One woman yelled; "You go, girl!" The guys were cheering her on, stomping to the lusty rhythms of the music. She held his brown legs, keeping him steady and sucked him to the shouts and whistles of her audience, the network of veins thickening in his stiff shaft as it plunged in and out between her lips. "Oh damn, baby," Wayne moaned at one point, his legs sagging. She was fascinated with the carnal response of the people watching them, faces in ecstasy, anguished expressions of near release and bliss. The sexual animal in them stirring. Undisguised lust. The women watched imagining they were her, and the men watched wishing they were him. Some of them were now kissing, feeling each other up or masturbating openly. She begged Wayne to enter her right there on the dance floor, throw one of her legs over his shoulder and penetrate her to the hilt. The clapping reached a peak when he started trembling, shooting his seed into her mouth, his thighs almost totally enclosed around her bobbing head. Totally aroused, she was sopping wet. She lifted a leg, took off her soiled panties and tossed them into a ring of excited Latin guys. One of them caught the underwear, yelling and pumping his fist in the air. He howled once more and covered his face with the drenched panties. Finished, she waved and walked off the dance floor side by side with her ashamed lover. Wayne almost left her after that. To this day, he never mentioned that decadent night. It never happened.

Her memory of one of her wildest nights slowly faded, and she was back in her old sterile married life. "Are you sure I can't convince you to stay home?" she asked cheerfully. "We could stay in bed like we used to do before the kids were born, eat snacks, read to each other and fool around. A day alone with just the two of us. No distractions. How does that sound?"

"No, baby, I've got to go and that's that." He sounded as if she was starting to annoy him with her insistence that he remain home.

Not budging from the bathroom doorway, she kept at him until he barked at her to leave him alone so he could get dressed. She watched him standing in his T-shirt before the sink, humming to himself as he brushed his teeth. He was slightly above-average height, moonfaced with gray eyes, curly salt-and-pepper hair, taut stomach, had all his own teeth and the most beautiful hands she'd ever seen on a man. And he was primping for some witch at his job. That pissed her off. It was as if he was happy to get away from her. Must be the damn secretary. Had to be something there. Her husband watched his reflection in the mirror above the sink, admiring his face as though he was still in the prime of his youth. He was nearly forty. There was a special care in the way he shaved his face, using the razor in swift, precise strokes to remove the night's stubble. She couldn't stop her mind from playing with the thought that he was doing all of this for the new young female in his office, trying to impress her.

"Are you still going to have time to drink coffee?" she asked with a hint of meanness in her words.

"Yes, if you can fix it in the next ten minutes," he said, smiling cleverly at himself in the glass before erasing his mustache with a few quick swipes of the blade. Without the mustache that he'd worn for more than fifteen years, he looked at least ten years younger, and that instantly brought a stinging rebuke from his wife.

He ignored her and went back into the bedroom, opening the closet to take out one of his gray suits. A white shirt, crisply starched, was laid out on the rumpled bed, along with clean underwear, a pair of black socks, and his red power tie. His black wingtips, which he'd shined to a glossy sheen the night before, were situated at the door to the hall, along with his briefcase. In six minutes, he dressed, slipped some galoshes over his shoes, put on his earmuffs and left without ever tasting a drop of coffee. If he was angry at her for not getting the coffee, he never showed any kind of displeasure, instead he was whistling a snappy Whitney Houston tune when he left. She couldn't figure him out. It was as if another man had taken possession of her husband's body, more confident, less moody, more at home in his skin, almost happy.

As soon as her husband closed the door, Joanne prepared the coffeepot for the two cups that would get her through the morning, the brew's rush a real necessity for her sanity. She weighed the events of the day so far, his peacock show, his good mood, and insistence to go to work. It all added up to bad news. Another woman, his secretary. But there had been troubling things going on between them in their supposedly fairy-tale marriage for some time.

She quickly called her best girlfriend, Francine, and asked her to drive over. Francine begged her to tell her what was wrong—was someone sick? Was it something with the kids? But she wouldn't give her an answer over the phone. A blizzard outside, and she had to appear in person to get the news. Three hours later, after a hair-raising drive on frozen city streets, her buddy arrived, cold and shivering. Joanne served her espresso, crullers and her suspicions about her husband.

"So what's up, girl?" Francine asked, watching her friend over the rim of her cup. Francine was a plus-sized woman who loved good food, good gossip and good sex.

"Wayne's fooling around." Joanne said it like it was a fact. The unadulterated truth.

"Honey, you've got to kidding me," her friend gasped, putting down the cup. "How do you know he's cheating? Did you catch him?"

"No, not yet but I've got a feeling that something's going down with him and his perky little secretary. I don't trust that hussy as far as I could throw her. She always answers his phone with this snide little nicey-nicey thing in her voice like she knows something that I don't know. She's all up in his business, girl. Whenever I call there if he has to work late, she answers the phone like she's the damn wife and I'm nobody. She runs his life. Whenever I get flowers or gifts from him, it's usually her that buys them. I can't stand her."

"Is that all you've got on him?"

"No, he's just different, acting different," Joanne said. "It's like he's in love."

"Well, I know you told me that you were having problems in the bedroom. Maybe that's what's got him crazy. Maybe he's having a midlife crisis."

Once Wayne called her frigid in a fit of anger when she wouldn't give him any. Frigid, hell! Her aunt told her there was no such thing as a frigid woman, just men who didn't know what to do in the bedroom. Lousy lovers. Some of it might be her fault, maybe not. One thing she never admitted to anyone, even to herself until a few months ago, was that she refused to give any man sexual power over her. She wouldn't let any man control her with his dick, no sir.

"How do you tell a man that you're not being satisfied?" Joanne asked aloud. "No man can handle that. Their egos are too big to hear that kind of truth."

"I guess but I don't have that problem," her friend replied. "Henry does the best he can, and I love him, so I work around it. With him, if I didn't play with myself during sex, I'd never have an orgasm. But that's ok. There's more to what we have than sex."

Joanne was not hearing any of it. She was determined to catch them in the act. The cheaters. She figured that they would slip up on a day like today, no one in the office. Her proposal to Francine was to drive into town and watch them, follow them and see what they did. They were probably the only ones there in the office, and she'd watch them when they left and then everything would be revealed.

"Drive all the way to the city in all this snow so you can snoop on them?" Francine exclaimed. "You've got to be kidding, girl. You're out of your mind. Don't be crazy."

Crazy or not, near lunch time, the two women found themselves parked a half a block from the office building where Wayne worked, sitting in a cold car, shivering. Twice on the way there, they almost skidded off icy roads, nearly turned back, but Joanne was determined to get there to see what she had to see. She was obsessed with catching her husband in the wrong. They would start the engine every twenty minutes and let the car warm up before they switched it off again. The hours passed slowly, and they waited and waited.

Finally, they saw the pair, Wayne and his secretary, come out of the building, their heads bent down to keep the howling wind and blowing snow from assaulting their faces. As they reached the corner, Joanne ordered her friend to follow them, slowly and carefully. Their car eased along in a creep, keeping their prey in sight until they ducked into a fancy bar two blocks from their job. Joanne suddenly jumped out of the car and ran recklessly across the street, with Francine trotting breathlessly behind her. The two women stood outside of the bar, watching the couple sitting at a cozy table, laughing and drinking.

"See how close they're sitting to each other," Joanne shrieked. "Don't tell me he's not doing her. I know he's screwing with her. I've seen enough. I knew it, I knew it. Let's go."

Back in the car, Joanne continued to rant about how much of a dog her husband was, now caught in the act. During her tirade, she flashed back to better times, to the two of them driving home from a day in the country, with the kids asleep in the back. She was sitting beside him, and his hand casually wandered over to her thigh and under her summer dress. His fingers worked their way under the elastic of her panties, into her, and played with her clit. She wiggled in her seat, pushing against his hand, moaning low, until one of the kids woke up and asked her when were they getting home.

"I'll let him have it when he gets home tonight," Joanne shouted. "I won't let him make a fool out of me with that slut. I can play rough too."

"But is that little scene at the bar enough to break up your home?" her friend asked. "Don't you think you're jumping to conclusions here?"

"Hell no," Joanne retorted. "I saw what I saw and that's enough for me. Take me home. I want him out by the weekend. Gone. I'll call his lying, cheating ass as soon as I get home. Don't mess with me. He doesn't know who he's fooling with here. Him and that little whore."

"What is this really about, Jo?" Francine asked. "Is this guilt? Is this about your little thing with your boss a few months ago? Is your conscience finally catching up with you?"

"No, that's different. I didn't rub his face in it like he's doing to me. He never even knew I stepped out on him. I kept everything cool."

Her affair. Her three-month affair with Michael, her boss at the language center. A thirty-year-old brother from Philly with a durable runner's build who spoke fluent Chinese, Russian, Portuguese, French and Italian. She remembered her breasts hanging over her lover's face and his teeth biting her nipples, hard then harder. That almost made her hit the roof. She felt comfortable with him sexually, something she had never experienced with any other man. He complimented her on her smooth, soft behind, her long legs and graceful swan like neck. Called her a real thoroughbred. He held her legs up high off the bed and kissed and lapped her lower lips until she screamed and made him stop. She wanted his dick and that alone. He'd thrust solidly into her body, with her hanging half off the bed, her head almost banging against the floor. The sheer male power of him. They made love in all kinds of positions, with their bodies in all manner of contortions—against the wall, on the floor, on the sofa, against the sink, on top of the kitchen table, in the shower, even out on the balcony in the night air. She couldn't get enough of him. Many times she'd start dressing, complaining that it was getting late and that she was expected home, but he'd lift up her skirt, either to kiss her between the legs or to insert a finger. And after that, it was back to bed. Once they finished, they lay there panting and laughing. Sometimes he'd eat her or suck one of her breasts hungrily while she called home to tell her husband that she'd be late. Working. Paperwork. Calls to make and last-minute odds and ends to clear up.

Before they drove away from the scene, Francine suggested that they wait and watch what the couple did next. When the supposed lovebirds came out of the bar and returned to work, she asked Joanne if she wanted to go up and really check out what they were doing in that empty office, all alone. Her friend agreed at first but thought the better of it upon further reflection. She knew she had always been extremely jealous and distrustful of her husband, to a fault. It was her Achilles' heel, her jealousy. It was irrational, powerful, and the controlling force in her emotional makeup. Something she'd fought during all of her relationships, a tendency to believe the worst of any man. Now when she had the chance to actually see the truth for herself, she balked, wondering what would happen to her if all of her suspicions were confirmed.

Francine, saying nothing, got out of the double-parked car and crossed the street again. She walked right past the security guard, who quickly asked her to sign in before going up. The signature only took a moment and then she stepped into the wood-paneled elevator for the ride to the tenth floor and Wayne's office. Quietly, she walked down the long hallway, looking for the sign that would tell her that she was in the right place. Halfway down the corridor, she located the door and gently worked the knob until it opened. There was nobody in the office that Francine could see upon entering, but the faint sounds of someone deep in the throes of hot sex caught her ear after a few steps. She tiptoed toward the song of sex, easing silently upon the door that was slightly ajar and peered in shock at the sight of Wayne pounding frantically into the wetness between the secretary's outstretched legs, her head thrown back, eyes closed and her hips swaying into his hard thrusts. Thank God that Joanne had decided not to come up. She tried to avert her eyes from the shameful sight but couldn't. Instead, Francine found herself standing there in the doorway, unzipping her jeans and massaging herself as the moans and sighs reached an unearthly pitch. Soon she was engulfed in sexual heat, and her legs buckled. How could Joanne let some hussy like this girl get her mitts on such a gorgeous hunk of male flesh like Wayne? she asked herself. As the pair of lovers eventually sagged against each other after a big orgasm, lost in the blissful fog that comes after climax, she stepped back and walked silently out of the office.

"Girl, they weren't doing nothing but talking and working on some damn account," Francine lied after returning to the car and an anxious friend. "But I think something could happen with them unless you step in. Don't be hasty. You can keep him with no trouble. All you have to do is to take care of business between the sheets. Give him an erotic evening he will never forget. You've got a good man, and there's no reason for you to throw him out so some woman who doesn't deserve him can get him."

"So they weren't doing anything?" Joanne couldn't believe it. She just knew they would be up there doing the nasty. But maybe Francine was right, maybe she was jumping to conclusions and letting her knack for jealousy get the best of her when it wasn't necessary. "Nothing at all. It was all business."

"You think I'm crazy for coming out here like this, don't you?" Joanne asked. "Tell the truth."

"No, I know you're crazy. But listen to me. You've got to stop being so self-centered, so selfish. You've got to think about somebody other than yourself. Let that man know that you want him, that you love him."

"So you're saying this is all my fault, right?"

"Joanne, I'm just saying that you should pay more attention to him at home and then you won't have to worry about a thing," Francine said, keeping a straight face. "Not a thing. Turn him out, girl. Rock his world, and he won't look at another woman."

"What should I do?" her friend asked, admitting that it had been too long since she put together an evening of romance and seduction. "I'm out of practice, Fran. Give me some tips."

"First we'll stop and pick up some champagne to get you guys in the mood," Francine said, laughing. "A little incense and candles. Some Barry White and Luther Vandross. Take a bubble bath, drink a glass of wine to get you relaxed before he gets home. Do something with your hair, make yourself up real pretty, get out that slinky lingerie you bought from Victoria's Secret and become the woman of his dreams. Then do your seductive Circe routine when he arrives. Make his nature rise, make him fall in love with you all over again. You can do it, girl. I know you can."

When Joanne got home, she followed her friend's instructions and ran a tub full of hot, steaming water, sprinkled some bath salts into it and poured in a few capfuls of bath oil. Stripping away her damp clothes, she sank into the perfumed water, feeling it soothe away the tension. Her hands cupped her wet, bubble-covered breasts. She thought back to the days when she didn't need a bra, before the birth of the kids. Instinctively, her fingers caressed her tingling body, moving hungrily over her and down into the water to her pubic hair, toying with the lips of her pussy and resting on the tip of her clitoris before sliding inside. She imagined Wayne making love to her, gently and expertly, caressing and kissing her, while she massaged her bud with a steady, demanding rhythm until the tremors of passion swept through her.

In the midst of her sexual reverie, she heard Wayne's key in the door, and her heart leaped. He called to her once to announce his arrival home, then took off his galoshes and heavy coat. His voice was cheery and upbeat. Time passed, and there was no response from his wife, so he concluded that she must be still angry from their morning argument. With this in mind, he sat warily on the sofa in the living room, took his daughter's tan Barbie doll from its hidden place under his butt and laid it carefully on the coffee table.

"Hello, sweetheart," Joanne said, walking sexily into the room carrying an ice bucket with a bottle of champagne peeking out. "I missed you all day. I'm so glad you're home, honey."

He looked at her with a quizzical expression, standing up to give his customary smooch on her cheek. Then he noticed what she wearing, a new silk red gown with thin spaghetti straps and a low tempting V-back. Absolutely nothing underneath, from what he could see. As she walked toward him, he enjoyed the enticing jiggle of her breasts under the silk and sensed his dick jump in anticipation. He also felt a moment of extreme guilt, a flashing image of his secretary wiggling underneath him, but quickly defeated it when his wife stepped into his arms and placed her warm arms around his neck. Her sizzling kiss, all lips and tongue, made his privates leap again and stiffen.

"What is this all about?" he asked. "What have you done naughty?"

"Nothing." She smiled weakly, passing him a glass of the bubbly. "I thought we should have a nice, romantic evening for once, especially with the kids gone. We don't have enough of them. I feel like I've been neglecting you lately, and I want to correct that, starting tonight."

"I'm game," he agreed, standing inches from her wanting lips.

She stepped away from him, lit the candles and incense before switching off the lights. Suddenly, the deep, rich voice of Barry White filled the room, setting the mood, as she slowly danced in front of him, taking off the gown inch by inch. He stood there, mesmerized by the hypnotic beauty of his wife, his Joanne, his senses inflamed by the sumptuous sight of her satiny flesh. His entire body became one huge erogenous zone while his eyes devoured the view of his wife bumping and grinding before him. Off came the thong panties she wore underneath the gown and a wicked smile played at the corners of his mouth. Damn, she was so hot! The carnality of her impromptu strip show reminded him how passionate and sensual his wife had once been before the children appeared and things settled into a rut.

"Oh, baby, I'd forgotten how sexy you really are," he mumbled, sipping the golden liquid before words. "Forgive me for not keeping up my end. I love you so much."

Cole Riley

His mouth met hers before she could get out an answer, and he led her to the bedroom, where his lips and tongue did their bewitching alchemy on her breasts, neck and inner thighs. Her senses were excited beyond the limit, toward an all-consuming desire that kept her cumming and cumming. She screamed that she couldn't wait much longer, she wanted to feel him inside her after she reciprocated by nipping on the tip of the swollen knob of his engorged dick. They switched places on the bed, into a sort of spooning to sixty-nine each other. Both curled up, lips upon the other's sex.

He stopped the teasing before he reached his peak, and righted himself, kneeling over her, rubbing his erect tool between her large breasts, hardening it even more between her cleavage. Now delirious with desire, his wife grabbed him by the shoulder and pushed him down, her other hand firmly around his dick. Her entire body screamed with expectation and wanting. She smiled when his large, hot rod entered her, the echoes of its throbbing deep within her. Her sex closed around him tightly, its muscles fighting to contain his complete length, but he withdrew and then sank even deeper into her. The way he made love to her was always so sweet, thoughtful, and the memory of their secret rhythms pushed her to open still wider to accommodate him farther into the back of her, against the nexus of nerves in the walls of her velvet pocket. And he hit them again and again, feeling her tense up, craving release. It slowly became too much, both of them totally lost in the rapture of their gyrations, and then she bit his neck, giving in to the roar of the sexual storm inside her. They clung to each other desperately, their arms locked around the other's body when the burst of shuddering sensation seized them, compelling them to quiver and shout in its praise.

Afterward, they lay naked on the bed, holding hands and calmly chatting. She still shuddered from the aftershocks of her orgasms, her skin glistening all over from the glow of sex. He sipped from her glass, stroking her hair while watching her. Without any prompting, she scooted to him and nestled herself in his embrace, her head with its wet hair damply clinging to her neck.

"Joanne, let's start over and recapture what we once had," her husband said, kissing her eyelids. "We're still good together. I forgive you for what you've done in the past. Your little indiscretions. I haven't been

92

an angel myself. We've both screwed up in our own way but that's all behind us. I love you, and I want to keep what we have alive. We deserve a second chance. What do you say, sweetheart?"

Somehow it didn't matter that he knew about her affair with her boss. It didn't matter that he had screwed up somehow. What did matter was that he was hers again, completely hers. And nothing would ever change that or threaten their love again. She took his face delicately in her hands and planted one long, passionate kiss on his lips, feeling the nearness of his body give her yet another rush of desire. They held each other close all night, smug and confident in their new-and-improved love, and slept like babies until the annoying noise of traffic on the street outside woke them the next morning.

HOW MR. WATSON'S KISSES MADE A DIFFERENCE

I'd been watching Mr. Watson for some time at the gym but I'd never approach him because he was the husband of my best friend. I always considered him the ideal husband and father to Irma's three boys. She always bragged about him, about how caring he was around the house, about how he was constantly at the school participating in activities there with the boys, about what a tiger he was in bed. In fact, the more she bragged about him, the more I wanted to try him out, the more aroused I became whenever I saw his pretty black self at the gym.

Since Mr. Watson joined the gym a few blocks from my job, I've become a regular gym rat, staying on that damn StairMaster for hours just so I can watch him lift weights, flex his pecs and strut around, displaying that marvelous muscle tone of his. One day recently after my workout, I grabbed up my towel, gloves and water bottle and went to the showers, still thinking of seeing Mr. Watson doing crunches with ease. That accounts for that incredible set of washboard abs he shows off for the women at the gym. There can't be one of them who wouldn't let him have his way with her, anything the brother wanted to do, no problem. And most of them were married like myself, with a decent, boring husband at home and children and bills. The usual family routine.

So I was in the shower, feeling the hot water soothe my aching muscles and tendons when I hear this low buzz of whispers and sighs behind me. I kept my eyes closed, the water was delightful, imagining that Mr. Watson was holding me in his massive arms from behind, his bulge pressing against my ass, and that rippling chest covering my wet back like a jacket of velvet muscle. Velvet muscle, right. When I finished my shower and walked out to my locker, I heard the buzzing again but ignored it, sitting on the bench to apply lotion. Suddenly, the women, some of them completely naked, ran back into the locker room, all worked up. I knew who they were talking about, because Mr. Watson had a tendency to walk around after his shower in just a thong, leaving nothing to the imagination. The Black Adonis. More pecs and definition than Arnold and Sylvester combined, with an ego to match.

"Girl, you missed a real show," Kuma, a workout friend of mine, said, fanning herself with one hand. A banana-hued sister, with her auburn hair in little twists, Kuma was a known eyeful and flirt to the men at the gym with her five-foot-six-inch frame of perfect curves and dips. "Man, how does Irma let him out of the house looking like that? I'd have his black ass chained to the couch. Ain't no way he should be running around loose looking like that? I'm serious."

I smiled, having seen the perfect specimen completely nude one day through his bathroom window. He was standing at the sink, face covered with shaving cream, with the razor raised to do damage. Unfortunately, I didn't get a chance to size him up on the real tip, window angle and all. But what I saw was enough to whet the appetite. Shortly after that, I started going to the gym like a religious fanatic to Sunday worship.

"You know, he's my neighbor," I said, flaunting my advantage. "I see him all the time."

"Do you have binoculars, girl?" she asked and burst out laughing.

At that moment, I thought about how our husbands, Irma and mine, were so different in personalities and temperament. Mr. Watson, the object of our affection, was outgoing, dominant, loud, all energy, a real Alpha male. Word was that he could party for days on end and never burn out. Craig, my husband, was just the opposite. He was steady, dependable, quiet, deliberate and usually wouldn't say anything unless he was asked. In fact, he was a man of few words, never saying anything unless he thought it was totally profound. They were as different as night and day, one an extrovert and the other an introvert. Yet, I must admit that his quiet manner was one of the major reasons I married Craig. I hate chatty, yakking men. Too female.

Another thing that sparked my interest in Mr. Watson was how Irma always bragged about him, not just to me but to all the girls. And you know how sisters can be, too much advertising will always start the wheels to spinning. Irma was always giving little parties for the girls, all her supposedly close friends, and they would be watching for Mr. Watson sightings the entire time. She must have known what she was doing by putting so much temptation so close to a virile, sexy beast like her man. I figured that they must have had some kind of arrangement where he did his thing and she agreed to look the other way. Everyone knew the man was always on the prowl. Always stalking fresh meat, new conquests. But if Irma knew something was going on with Mr. Watson, she never let on. Maybe her motto was that she didn't care what he did in the streets, as long as he came home every night. A lot of women married to pretty men do just that.

One afternoon while Irma and I sat sipping Bloody Marys on her patio, I got my first real clue as to what their marriage was really like. She, somewhat zonked on drinks, began talking about her husband in a way that she never had before, and I was all ears.

"Is he a good lover, Irma?" I asked, not expecting a detailed answer.

"Oh, yes," she chirped. "Gary's like a bull in the sack. He never tires or runs out of steam, wears me out all the time. Girl, I'm sore for days after he gets done with me. But you know one thing? He doesn't like talking afterward. He goes right to sleep, maybe it's because he's not terribly smart. I doubt he's ever cracked a book, but that's not why I married him in the first place."

"Do you ever worry about him out there with all of that available female flesh?" I asked next, looking over her shoulder for him. "Do you ever worry he'll stray?"

"No, I can't worry about that or I'd go crazy," she replied, sipping from her glass. "I know he fools around. He goes through women like socks. As long as he doesn't bring any diseases home, I really don't care what he does. And if I did, what could I do about it? A man's going to do what a man's going to do. Any woman who thinks she can stop him from doing it is a fool. You just can't worry about that."

"See, I couldn't do what you do," I said. "I'd be crazy in two days. I know I'm suspicious. I always think the worst, mainly because I know men."

She stood, taking her half-empty glass with her. "You don't have to worry about that with Craig. He's Mr. Reliable. A good husband and family man. You're lucky."

"Have you ever been unfaithful to him?"

"Heck no, he's more than enough man for me. Why would I go out there and jeopardize everything I've got here. He's a good provider, a lot of fun and keeps me amused."

Keeps me amused. I was thinking about that the other day when I was at the workout room sign-in desk as Mr. Watson walked past, with a bevy of young women trailing him as if he were the Pied Piper. I was looking at the roster for the line where I'd sign my name. He came up beside me and stopped, smiling. I expected him to say something but he didn't. Later as I was taking the elevator to the floor where my yoga class was held, he got in with me, moving real close before making some small talk.

"I've always wanted to talk to you but I was afraid of how that might look with you being my wife's friend and all," he said with a great deal of charm. "I think you're one of the most beautiful women in this town. You don't know how gorgeous you really are, do you?"

I didn't answer but I smiled shyly. Is this how he did it? Is this how he lured those other women? All pearly-white teeth and hard muscle.

"I need someone to talk to," he said with a serious expression on his face. "It's about Irma and myself, our marriage. She seems to have lost interest in sex. We barely touch anymore. What am I supposed to do?"

"Have you talked to her about it?" I asked, knowing exactly where this line of talk was headed. He was setting up a rationale for making a play for me and giving me some reasons to consent to whatever he had in mind.

97

"Yes, I have but she doesn't say anything," he replied, pressing the button for the elevator to ascend to the roof. "I guess there are several ways I could handle this, but I don't know which one would resolve things between us. A friend of mine, a woman, said the best way would be to get a lover on the side, someone who understands what it was like to be in an unsatisfying marriage, and that way both of us would solve our problems. See, when you get married, you think I'm going to be with this person for life but little do you know that no one person can meet all of your needs. And you're supposed to be faithful even if it means that you suffer. Are you satisfied with your marriage?"

I stepped back from him. "We have our share of problems. Most marriages do but you try to remain faithful and work things out. I like being married."

" Sounds like some Moral Majority bullshit," he said, staring at me with his intense eyes. "I think marriage is overrated. You live with the same person and make love to them every day, every year, the same way, nothing new. You get bored. An affair can spice things up."

The elevator was passing floors and nearing the door to the roof. I was sweating, afraid of this hulking man but very excited by the possibility of being with him sexually. "So you take a lover, have your fun and hope you're not found out," I said solemnly. "You believe that if you do it right and be careful, then you'll never be discovered. You can have your cake and eat it too. You lie to yourself that you're making the pair of you happy by stepping outside of your marriage. And you even bring a few new tricks home with you to add a little more uumph to your sex life with the wife. But how can it ever be the same if you're sharing yourself with someone else? And what happens if you're caught?"

"She knows I screw around," he said proudly. "What can she do? She accepts it. I'm a man. I didn't stop being that when I got married."

The elevator stopped on the roof, and he grabbed my hand and led me out into a small decorated shed that was alive with the sweet fragrance of flowers. He put his other hand on my cheek, looking deeply into my eyes, then stepped into me, kissing me full on the lips. That shocked me, and my heart raced when I discovered myself returning his kisses, giving him tongue, parting my lips to receive him deep into my mouth. I felt a sexual excitement I had not experienced in years. It was like being a young girl again, doing something naughty, forbidden, taboo. In my head, I kept repeating: *This is not your husband, this is not your husband. You should stop this right now.* But I couldn't. I could feel the moisture starting to collect in my panties, and soon he reached down into the elastic of my exercise suit and touched me there. Slowly, skillfully, evilly.

In no time, he removed my clothes, and his strong, muscular body covered mine. Even now I remember his large purple lips on me, his snake like tongue melting my resolve with its every flick against my clit, addicting me to him in a way that would make it extremely difficult for me to ever be the same with my husband. He was a master at this, taking his time, not rushing it as if it were a chore. He wanted to eat me, he loved eating me, something my husband avoided like the plague. Each stroke of his tongue got me hotter and hotter as I wiggled and pushed against his face, wanting more of it.

What made it all even worse was that he talked to me while he made love to me, another thing my husband never did. I understood now why Irma put up with his mess.

"Experience me, sweetness, enjoy this," he cooed into the electrified folds of my sex. "I want to share this with you, I want us to be connected forever. I've wanted to do this for so long, so very long."

My mind was clouded from his expert touch, his artful tongue. "Oh, my God, what are you doing to me?" I tried to make sense of what I was doing. He took away my reason by kissing every inch of my body, paying more attention of my breasts, my nipples than my husband ever had. While he sucked and licked my breasts, he took his thumb and middle finger and tenderly stroked the bud nestled at my opening, caressing the top of it until my back arched up into the air involuntarily.

Suddenly, he stopped, watching me squirm on the floor before him, then his hand reached for his pants. I watched him put the condom on the tip of his dick and carefully smooth it down. "We can't have any accidents, can we?" he said, grinning. This was truly a man who had made cheating an art form, a real pro.

He parted my legs a bit more and slowly slid into me, and pulled himself out. I guess he wanted to see my juice covering the latex before he went back to work. Once we got going, I worked my hips against him, rocking back and forth so I could feel him all the way up in me, striking that spot. Believe me, it was never like this with my husband. Wrapping my legs around his back, I ordered him to go deeper still, to make me cum. I begged him for it in a voice I didn't recognize. We were grinding together in that heat where your mind goes blank—that white flash, you know what I mean—and then you feel that sensation coming, way in the back of your pussy, the sudden warmth. Getting closer, closer and closer. I reached down and stroked his balls, touching that space between his sac and his anus. He moved even harder against me, his hands covering both cheeks of my behind, hoisting me up into the air. And that warmth returned, building quicker this time, more intense than ever. I felt totally out of control.

"You can take me any way you want," I said breathlessly. Another first. "Any way."

He said nothing, just varying his thrusts, shallow ones that titillated all of the nerves near the opening of my sex, then deeper ones that filled the full depth of me. He was not especially long but extremely thick, and this caused a popping sound whenever he pulled back. Then he laid me on my side and went back into me with such vigor that I became lightheaded. I heard myself saying to him: "Yes, sugar, take all of it, get up in it, tell me how you want it, tell me." I never talk when I have sex. Never. This wasn't like me at all. But this was something that was not the usual thing in my life. He groaned when I tightened myself around his staff, and we held each other close until he hit something again, and I felt myself cum with him moving slowly inside me. I screamed out his name, grabbed him, holding him against me with all of my strength. Every woman, or at least most, know what that feeling is like when you cum so hard and feel like you don't know when one of you ends and the other begins. We stopped to regain our senses and rest, but I started touching him again, licking his dick and playing with his balls. I couldn't get enough of him.

I realized right at that moment that I had never really been in love before, not with any man, not even with my husband. Somehow everything was shuffled around, and my marriage didn't make much sense after that incident in the shed. We met for four more times after that, but I kept my marriage going. At night, I would lie still in our bed, letting my husband do the same things to me that he had done for our whole time together. I was a great actress, sometimes crying out his name as I remembered what it had been like with Mr. Watson, sometimes scooting away from him on the bed as if he were going to kill me with passion if he sexed me anymore. Sometimes I wondered how many women fake it like that just to keep their stable home and family going.

But it never stopped me from thinking of him, Mr. Watson, and his kisses and his touch. He got mad at me because I would quiz him about his marriage, what his wife was like in bed, what things she did. But he stopped answering me after a while. He said he didn't want to bring "that thing," his futile marriage, into what we had together. Still, I would sometimes look through the window at their house and imagine his fingers inside her, his lips at the down of her throat, his tongue creeping craftily along the throbbing nerves of her thighs. I imagined him taking her with force, then slowing the pace down to totally take her to rapture. I imagined him telling her that she was the only woman for him, that he was glad that she was in his life, that he could love only her. How many of us say those things after just spending a few hours with someone else? What does it take to continue that kind of lie for years? I wanted him to tell her that he was leaving her, that he had met someone that he could not live without. If he did that, I knew I'd leave my husband, my kids, my home, my life in a heartbeat. I would do it and not look back. But I knew he never would do that, and I would never have to make that horrible choice.

In the middle of the last night when we were together, just before I laid my head on his chest to sleep for a little while before we showered and went to do our bit of theater at our respective homes, I whispered cattily into his ear: "Mr. Watson, what if I went over and had a little talk with the missus? If Irma threw you out, would you go away with me? If you love me as much as you say you do, could you walk away from her and the kids to be with me?"

He pretended to be asleep and never replied. But I could see his eyelids flickering in the mirror's reflection, but I didn't confront him on it. Now when he sees me, he either looks the other way or pretends I don't exist. Even my husband commented on how cool and remote Mr. Watson has become. How soon they forget, huh?

IRRESISTIBLE

Lightning crackled in long twisted bolts of illumination across the endless stretches of fertile, flat land in the distance. This was Kansas, the fabled territory of Oz, Dorothy and her little dog, Toto.

She kept her bloodshot eyes on the winding asphalt road ahead of her, trying to beat the rain that the dark clouds overhead promised would come. On both sides of the old Dodge, there were golden lakes of grain as far as one could see, with an occasional farmhouse or silo dotting the line of the horizon. The car's motor coughed, rattled and spat as she pushed it to the limits of its endurance, attempting to get to some kind of lodging before nightfall.

Now, she spent much of her time spreading the Gospel of the Lord, zigzagging across states, teaching the Holy Word wherever anyone would allow her to use their vacant field or building. Kansas was the fourth state on her current tour across the vast Midwest. It was a grueling business. Sometimes a good neighbor, one of her newly converted lambs, would take mercy on her and invite her to take a spare room rather than travel on the road in the dark. Sometimes she was not so lucky and would have to sleep in her car. Since she left Chicago three weeks ago, she'd work most of the towns around Kansas City, everywhere from Lawrence, Overland City, Topeka, all the way out to Emporia. Tonight, with luck, she'd stop in Iola, a small place in the middle of nowhere.

Before God, there was her addiction to men. Always men. Of all shapes and sizes. She was brought to New York City more than ten years ago to audition at a modeling agency after a scout had seen her photo in one of the local papers in Detroit, a cheesy shot of her standing next to a new Ford. Her mother watched her like a hawk during that first stay in the big city, never letting her daughter out of her sight. The older woman lectured her endlessly about the perils of being seventeen in a metropolis like New York City without anybody to protect or guide her. Oh, the temptations and sins that awaited her. Everybody that saw her told her how beautiful she was, a combination of Cindy Crawford, Iman and Veronica Webb. Something exotic, something original. She had no idea how obsessed with beauty everybody, the entire society, was until she listened to her handlers and her mother discuss how much her face and body would bring doing runway and print work in Europe.

Often she wondered what her engineer father would have thought if he'd lived to see her on her way to fame and fortune. He'd been killed instantly on her tenth birthday when a car driven by a teenager, hopped up on three 40s of chilled malt liquor, lost control of his vehicle. It jumped the curb and ran him down. It was a loss that left a void in her that would never be filled. And yes, she was tall, pretty, clever and healthy, but was she worth the thousands of dollars they paid her hourly to walk up and down in front of gawking people. Her mother continually cautioned her that looks didn't last. Take advantage of them while you can. Nothing lasts forever. That's our only guarantee in life, her mother always concluded her beauty speech with this little pearl of wisdom.

Beauty carries such a heavy price at times. Nobody would imagine that she spent so many weekends alone in a darkened room in front of a television. Nobody would imagine she'd been dumped more than once by men intimidated by her looks or dreams. Nobody would imagine how often guys had wooed her with lofty promises of fidelity only to flee at the first note of commitment or real intimacy. No, she'd learned that it was so fleeting, the magazine covers, the chic nightlife, the fancy vacations, the high life. At nineteen, she was a has-been, burned out, with a serious cocaine habit and memories of an Italian boyfriend, Mario, who overdosed on heroin. The good times were behind her. When things got bad, her mother deserted her, just like she knew she would.

Life in the fast lane was too fast. Before Mario died, there was the one night that damaged her trust of men forever. She came home from a photo shoot to a living room where her boyfriend sat with another girl, Laura, a model he'd been working with for a session at *Elle* magazine. The shock on her face intensified when she saw the yellow girl was totally nude, except for the pale imprints where her bikini had once been. Her man was dressed only in his boxer-briefs. They were smoking joints on the bed, twisted around each other, and giggling. When she entered the room, they didn't stop what they were doing, instead Laura began inspecting Mario's stiff cock and playing with his tight sac of seed underneath with one finger. Following five deep puffs of the potent ganja, she felt completely buzzed and let them undress her, and soon Laura's head was between her legs, her big, round yellow behind up in the air. Mario slid below Laura's shiny crevice, tonguing her, his face moving in a slow rotation against her wetness. After a while, they changed places, taking a few more tokes, then Laura started sucking Mario's dick, holding it like a lollipop, feeling its pulse, feeling it thicken. She was touching herself at the same time, burying three fingers inside her dripping sex, as she took him all the way inside her mouth, causing him to growl low in his throat. For her, it was all like a dream, fuzzy and disjointed. It seemed as if she was watching herself in a strange porno movie until the three of them wound up on the sofa, with her on her knees licking Laura's pussy and Mario opening her legs as far as they could go, to seize her from behind. He cupped her firm butt cheeks, inserted his wiggling finger into her rear tightness while he sucked and stroked her engorged clit. His mouth left her trembling along her spine, down her long legs. It was the madness of it all, the way she felt his tongue everywhere at once, his grunts muffled by her flesh, her mouth around Laura's drenched labia. Laura's head flew back as bolts of sensation took possession of her. Suddenly, Mario positioned both of them with their faces toward the wall, their butts exposed for his touch and kisses. Finally, he rubbed his brick-hardness against both of their openings, teasing them until their legs buckled. Then he was inside them, alternating, moving like a rhythm machine harder and harder in each one, showing incredible stamina and skill. She could feel her juices running down the backs of her legs. He finished up riding her while Laura licked her tender breasts until he pulled out, shooting jism all along her back. Afterward, Laura tried to kiss her on the mouth but she turned her head. She was still tingling from the pounding. Laura, angry at the rejection, dug her long fingernails into the softness of her shoulders and back, raking them in three quick motions that left her bleeding. Laura then yelled she hated her and ran to the bathroom to put on her clothes. Sheer sadism. That was the last she saw of Laura.

Ten years later, all of her big dreams of becoming a hotshot actress with a big-time movie career had evaporated, because the drugs had left their mark on her looks. The little cutie-pie girl from Detroit, who had been transformed into a supermodel by a brigade of agents, stylists and photographers, was long gone. In her place, she was now an older, wiser and sober woman determined to redeem herself, to find redemption in this world before going on to the next one. Turning her life around was not easy. It took the near-death experience of an overdose at an after party in the back room at Cosmos, a trendy Soho nightclub, to bring her to the Lord. That autumn night, she'd been snorting coke for more than six hours straight when her nose started to bleed, and her heart began racing as if she had just finished the New York Marathon. Disoriented, she tried to get to the ladies' room, thinking she'd splash water on her beautiful face, when everything went black, and the floor came up to smack her in the mouth. A short time later, she was loaded in the back of an ambulance and rushed to St. Vincent's Hospital where doctors twice shocked her back to life after her heart shut down.

While she was fighting for her life, she saw herself outstretched on the gurney, with the doctors and nurses fighting to bring her back. Nothing they did seemed to work. Her father, dressed in his usual splendor, gave her an orchid from his suit lapel and whispered to her that it was now her choice. "Lizzie, you can live or you can die." There was a sly smile on his long, narrow face that she would never forget. "Your choice." Dead or alive. That night, she chose life. That night, she found the Lord. And she'd been working for Him every day since.

On the highway headed for the next town, she plowed ahead as the sky grew darker, letting the memories of a troubled past play quietly and quickly across the screen of her mind. She reached for a can of soda on the front seat, taking her eyes off the road for only a second. A slender figure suddenly popped up in front of her car just as she glanced up. The car's brakes screamed loudly, and she lurched to a stop scant inches from the man, who leaped back out of harm's way.

He stuck his head in the window of her car. "Lady, can you give me a lift to the next gas station? My car's up there ahead about two miles, out of gas. It looks like it's about to rain, and you're the first car I've seen in about an hour."

She looked him over carefully. A woman alone had to be cautious about picking up a hitchhiker or supposedly stranded motorist on the road. Covered with dust, he still appeared not to be the type that would cause any problems. Tall and slim, the man was dressed in a dark suit, shirt and tie, but wore sneakers. That worried her. His head was bald, and his body appeared to be quite firm under the cloak of the suit. It was his face that captivated her, unwrinkled and without any sign of the ravages of time. He wore the face of a child, open, innocent and pleasant to look at. She calculated his age to be somewhere in his early twenties.

She motioned for him to get in, which he did after swatting some of the dust from his clothes. "So where were you headed?"

"Redding, someplace, not even on the map." He stuck his hand into his shirt for a cigarette, but left it there when he saw the scowl on her face.

"Are you from there, this Redding?" she asked, keeping him in her line of sight.

"No, I'm just driving back from Kansas City from a job interview," he said almost cheerily. "A salesman job. I don't know if I got it. The guy said he'd call me in four days."

"I was just in Kansas City a few days ago," she said flatly, watching an airplane dust a field far off in the distance, swooping down out of the clouds to release its load of insecticide.

"What do you do?" the man asked, reaching absently for the pack of cigarettes again. "Do you live in Kansas City?"

She laughed and swerved to avoid something on the road, then straightened out the wheel. "I'm an evangelist. I travel around the country, teaching the Word of God."

"That must be pretty tough on your family, with you on the road all the time," he said. "What does your husband say about you driving all around preaching?"

"I"m not married," she replied. "I'm too busy for that kind of thing."

"That's odd. I thought all women wanted a husband, family and a home. It seems like the normal thing to do. Surely God wouldn't mind if you took yourself a man. It doesn't seem right for a person to go through this world alone. Without love."

"Well, my personal life takes second place to the work of God," she said, thinking about what he'd just said. "Sometimes it's not about what you want, but what He wants. He wants me to serve Him, taking his Word to sinners wherever I find them."

He laughed and said he'd been rude. "My name is Ray, Ray Draper, originally of Abilene and now of Redding. What's yours, lady?"

"Reverend Elizabeth Little," she answered. "Pleased to meet you."

"Reverend Liz, answer me this," Ray began, choosing his words with great care. "Do you ever miss men? Do you ever miss being loved and adored by a man?"

Sure, she missed it. Not that she'd ever tell him what it was like, sleeping in a different bed every night, with your body throbbing and aching from the lack of touch. It had been so long since she'd been with a man. Maybe six years. Maybe she'd forgotten what to do if the opportunity ever arose. And then there was the matter of her Calling, her ministry, that Divine business that left no room for indulging the flesh. If she strayed from the path and took herself a lover, who could ever say that she was a true disciple of the Lord. He'd saved her once, and she owed Him. Maybe this young man was a test of her faith, of her resolve, and she couldn't let herself be swayed by temptation.

"I've lived a full life and tasted every fruit," she said. "But that was all before I found the Lord. That"s all behind me now."

"It's sad." He said it like he pitied her. "Your God won't let you be a woman. I know people who worship or preach the Bible, and they live a good, normal life without denying themselves anything. I don't think they're evil people or anything."

"Everyone has their way of serving the Master," she said, pulling into the gas station, which seemed to suddenly appear out of nowhere. "This is my way of serving Him. I don't question Him."

"How do you know this is what He wants you to do?" he asked her, watching the man at the gas pump take a fistful of cash from another man in a truck. "You might have it all wrong. It sounds to me like you're punishing yourself for something."

She wanted to answer the man but he jumped out of the car and walked over to the gas station attendant, who appeared to know him. As she watched him, they started quarreling and the attendant took a swing at her passenger, who quickly knocked the guy down with a punch to the face. Then he went through the man's pockets before taking the money from his hand. She revved up the engine to pull away but Ray ran in front of her car, waving his hands. There was a gun in one of them. He pointed it at her, and she lifted her foot off the gas pedal. He walked around to her side of the car and got in, pushing her into the passenger side.

"Why did you do that?" she asked, fighting down her hysteria. "Why did you hit him like that?"

"He owed me some money. Also, my wife and kids ran off with him. He's lucky I didn't kill him. That's what I came up here to do, kill him. He got off easy, I think."

"Where are you taking me?" she asked as he pulled off, back on the road.

He didn't answer her. The car sped over the road for almost two miles before he turned into an alley behind an old roadhouse. They barely made it inside before it started to rain, a downpour. She watched his hand with the gun and wondered whether she could make a run for it. Her mouth tasted like copper, full of fear. At that moment, she remembered that there had been no deserted car on their way to the gas station. What a fool she had been!

No sooner had he settled in the room than he found a bottle of Scotch in one of the cupboards. It was almost full. He brought out two glasses and offered her one. She shook her head but he still held out the glass. His request that she join him in a drink was not polite; it was an order. Her body shook while she stared at him pouring her drink. This was a moment she'd feared for much of her time on the road. Many nights she'd pass a tavern or roadhouse during her travels, and it took every bit of her inner strength to keep going. Now she had no choice.

"You must have some past to be so scared of everything," he said, motioning for her to drink up. "What are you afraid of?"

"Myself. You wouldn't understand that. I've seen your kind of man before."

"What kind of man is that?" he asked, gulping down the last of his spirits.

"The kind of man who no longer believes in anything, not even in himself," she said. "The kind of man who wants to corrupt and poison everything he touches. Am I right?"

"Maybe," he muttered and covered his face with his hands. He seemed to be crying. Maybe it was the liquor, maybe it was genuine remorse and regret for the life he'd lived.

He said nothing else and continued to drink until he became sleepy. She drank one last drink with him and went to the bathroom where she stripped down to her blouse and panties, showered and washed her hair. At first, she wondered what he might do to her, but then she dismissed her fear and surrendered to the gentle spray of water. God was with her. No harm could come to her, not with him by her side. When she returned, he said she could have the bed, and the sofa would be his for the night. He promised her there would be no funny stuff. It didn't take long for her to fall asleep. He got up and walked to the bedroom door and stood there, listening to her soft breathing, watching her lying on her side.

He could see that Elizabeth was truly a splendid woman for a beauty nearing thirty-five, with a pleasing face, great legs and a magnificent, mature set of breasts. The temptation to satisfy his curiosity was so intense that he turned to leave but did not. Instead he knelt by her bed, and moved his hand lightly along the length of her exposed leg. He continued his explorations of her warm flesh until she sighed in her slumber and flipped on her other side, turning her rear to him. Carefully, he slid under the sheets next to her, still in his underwear, and as soon as his skin touched hers, he felt himself get hard. She was now awake, pre-

110

tending to be deep in sleep but every inch of her body was sensitized to his presence. There was no doubt that she wanted him, the first man she'd laid in bed with for longer than she could remember. Far too long.

Somewhere in the room was the solitary glow of a burning candle. Fortunately, he was not the manner of man who approached lovemaking as a chore to be finished as quickly as possible. His fingers hoisted the back of her blouse, gently unsnapped her bra, then massaged the softness of her shoulders, back and the nape of her neck. It was growing more difficult for her to continue her Sleeping Beauty act, especially when she felt his patient kisses blaze along her spine, on the rise and ebb of her hips and the satin mounds of her rear. His intrusive fingers, his kissing and cuddling, fueling the pitched battle between her desire and virtue. He smiled to himself because her body responded although she fought every impulse to make his task of seduction any easier. For a moment, she barely opened her eyes to drink in his body in shadow, him hunched over her with his distended spear of skin in hand, searching for entry between her unyielding lips. When he put her legs over his shoulders, he moaned at the first sampling of the fist-tight feeling of her tunnel, so narrow that it felt like breaking a disobedient hymen, almost virginal. He moved his hips up and down slowly, building her passion skillfully like a campfire, and when he almost slipped out, she twisted under him to hold him fast within her. She swallowed hard with each penetration of his dick, shivering but never withdrawing from the power of his thrusts. Something happened inside her. All of the inhibitions in her life no longer mattered. Only his lips soft against her skin mattered, only the length of his rigid cock inside her mattered. A real man. Not fantasy but real. The blood roared within his veins, his dick puffed up to a size where it hurt him to be in her, but he couldn't help himself with the background music of her moaning and talking filthy to him. He felt his seed rise and fill his balls yet he could not come, and she bucked and rolled in frustration on the bed after he withdrew from her without warning.

With a graceful motion, he lifted from the bed, carried her kicking to the bathroom where he placed her against the sink, facing away from him. Now he climbed on her, gripping her around the waist as if frightened of being thrown, and danced into her with gyrating hips. There was a touch of something urgent and hysterical in their second coupling. In the midst of her arousal, she confessed breathlessly to him that she'd wanted him all night and said little else while he plunged into her deep, propelling her to unimaginable ecstasy. She was amazed at how her pussy adjusted to his size, swallowing him to the nest of wiry hair at the base of his organ. Now at last she felt like a real woman, felt no longer a prisoner of her past. The rolling of his pelvis against her bottom excited her passions in a way she'd never known in her mature years, into a rapture that had been erased from her mind as the years went by. This unsuspecting man, she knew at that moment, had resurrected all of the emotions pent up by layers of deception, disillusionment and disappointment. In the whirlwind of her lust, she bit her lip and matched the fury of his movements, dancing back into him with each new spasm of pleasure that seized her. He shouted and sagged into the wall behind her, his cock leaking fluid down his quivering leg. She leaned over and sucked him until the last drop of his nectar had been extracted. Afterward, relishing the wonderful feeling of intimacy between them, they stayed in their individual poses, in the tiny cell of the bathroom, waiting for their hearts to quiet.

He smiled wickedly. "I know you won't stay with me. Right?"

How could she answer him? Sure, she was grateful for what he had given but there was no future between them. His face wore an odd hurt expression. She flinched when he politely took her hand gallantly, kissed it and begged her to stay with him. No answer existed for his questions. How could she explain her gratitude for what he had revealed to her with every thrust, every penetration? In her heart, she felt a tenderness for this stranger who had revived her sensuality, given it back to her in a way, but fought down an urge to surrender to him and submit to his every wish and command. She answered his probing eyes and questions by putting her arms around his neck, kissing his serious face, and crying as she never had for any other man.

They talked for hours in the darkness, side by side on the bed. Sleep finally came to them both. The sound of a car pulling up outside awoke them and soon there was a hard knock at the door. Ray slid on a shirt, hopped into his jeans and padded barefoot toward the living room. She sat up on the bed, grabbing for her blouse to cover her nakedness. Two

112

beefy white policemen stood in the doorway, quizzing Ray about his whereabouts the previous day, ultimately informing him that he was under arrest. Ray protested but to no avail. She sighed at the terrifying vision of her lover handcuffed by the officers, his massive muscular chest gleaming with sweat.

One of the officers found her purse on the sofa and fished around inside it. "You don't care who you screw, do you, Miss Little?"

Almost instantly, she was struck by the compulsion to laugh. With all of the eyes of the men fixed on her shapely frame, she faced them with a wild look in her stare, laughing maniacally while she opened her blouse and adjusted her bra over her full breasts. Still laughing, she sat down and pulled her dress over her legs, giving the voyeurs a long peek of her sex. They fidgeted, uneasy with the tantalizing spectacle of the woman. She felt another surge of laughter rising inside her.

"Boys," she said in a sultry voice, "you better behave, or you'll get in some real trouble. Take your prisoner and go. Bye, Ray. Thank you, sweetheart, for a really wonderful evening."

She was getting wet all over again, just thinking of the joys of the previous night, just imagining what was behind the tortured stares of the white officers. Nobody had ever reached so deep down into the center of her before, not like Ray had. The frigid evangelist's torrid night of sin and vice. Her astonishing fall from Divine grace.

"What did I tell you, Reverend Liz," Ray said as the men marched him down the path to the police car. "I screw up everything, tarnish everybody and everything around me. That"s what I do best. Screw up. I'm sorry for all this."

Just the roughneck sound of his manly voice caressed something in her, made her nipples erect again. "Ray, you're much too hard on yourself," she said. It was the last words she would ever say to her miracle lover bound for jail.

She remained in the doorway until the car was just a dot on the highway. "You don't care who you screw, do you, Miss Little?" That nonsense remark by the cracker officer only made her want to laugh again, only made her want to return to the tousled bed and pleasure herself once more. She realized she couldn't wait for them to leave so she could touch herself and relieve the taut coil of sexual tension throbbing between her legs. Ray really sparked something inside her. One thing was for sure, she would never deny herself again, not in this life. And to tell the truth, there was no way she could drive on the highway burning up from her need, feeling like this, all pent up again. Not all day. The woman in her was alive, awake. Armed with this glorious knowledge, Elizabeth Little started laughing again, laughing until her entire body shook from the force of it. Certainly the Lord wouldn't deny her this small moment of bliss.

MORE THAN YOU KNOW

Walking home under the stairs, holding hands, neither of us said much. I remembered how much my life had changed in the past year. When I met Roger, my honey man. Sometimes we go for walks like this on Sundays, that's the only day I have off. We're just pleased to be in each other's company, enjoying the quick bursts of talk as much as the long stretches of silence. There are times when we rarely leave the house. Tonight he laughed and told me he loves watching me walk from behind. He loves my pear-shaped, curvy backside. Most black men tend to be butt men like him, except my ex-husband, who loved big, melon-sized breasts, like white guys. The top-heavy blond, ditzy Pamela Anderson types. My ex was the silicone-implant king, drooling over them, living at strip bars where women with fake tits were plentiful. But enough about that fool and the past. This is about Roger.

Sometimes, like today, Roger won't let me leave the bed. He pushed me back on it and asked me to spread my legs so he can take a Polaroid picture of my pussy. When he took four shots of it, he laid them across a pillow and kissed each one. Said he would carry them around with him all day while he made the rounds of the neighborhood bars in Harlem. He's a nut. He constantly takes pictures of my face, my butt and my pussy. I wonder what he thinks of my legs.

Crawling across the carpeted floor, he moved to the edge of the bed and took my legs, joking I was suppressing my wild side, before he talked me into watching his fingers disappear inside me. I laid back and opened wider to let his digits have more freedom of movement, even lifting my rear up higher so his middle finger could vanish into the tight pucker of my backside. My pussy hungered for more than fingers. I moaned, pushing harder against his hand, which penetrated me, resisting the temptation to use my own hands to open the plump folds of my sex so he could find yet another pleasure spot in there. Just when I hit my orgasm, his tongue discovered my clit, that thumb of crackling nerves at the top of my wet cave, leaving it bigger and more sensitive than it has ever been. The combined simulation of his mouth and breath left me weak with sensual feeling, left me totally vulnerable to his every wish and urge. But he was not done. He kissed and sucked my stockinged feet, licking my toes through the sheer nylon, and tonguing my insoles and ankles. Another special Polaroid moment. No man had ever done these things to me. We decided to pick up this game after I got home from work.

I've been a cabbie for more than ten years and seen about everything out there to be seen. Cabbie No. 603. The guys tease me because I'm the only pretty woman working out of this garage. They've nicknamed me "Frenchie" because of my dark Afro-Creole looks and my outlandish outfits. The night supervisor said the other day that I looked like I was going out to snag me a man rather than to work. He calls my outfits "coochie clothes." Tight pants, low-cut blouses, even hot pants in the summer. I can feel the men's eyes on my behind when I walk out to the office, their looks like itchy hands on the curve of my butt, their blood starting to percolate. Hell, look all you want but touching is out. What woman doesn't want to be checked out? Those looks let you know you're still hot, still got it. When the guys stop looking, that's when you worry.

The other night, I was tired even before I went on the clock. I paid the owner his cut for the use of the car for the night, filled the tank with gas. I've always wanted my own cab but the price of a medallion was just high and without that, you missed out on the prime fares in midtown and the swank neighborhoods like Sutton Place, Park Avenue and all that. Wiped out. My wary thirty-four-year-old body still ached

116

from sitting behind the wheel for more than twelve hours the previous day, but it was starting to make a comeback.

At seventeen, I ran away from home, took the Greyhound bus from down South, from outside of Lafayette, Louisiana, north to the Promised Land. Some Promised Land. In my fantasies, I imagined New York City to be the City of Gold, especially seeing the towering, glittering skyscrapers of Manhattan on the postcards Cousin Clem sent home after a visit. Once I got here, it was not the way I thought it would be. This Paradise possessed another side, a darker, more vile side. I started hacking, driving a cab, in my late twenties to help bring some added cash into the house when my husband got laid off over at UPS. The thought of these more sinister elements of the city crosses my mind every time I pull back the bullet-proof Plexiglas partition and take the fare from a customer on a darkened street. Would I get robbed? Would the robber be content to just take my money? Would the robber take my life as well? Now, it wasn't enough for the robbers to rob you, they had to shoot you, too, and many of my friends in the business quit rather than risk getting killed. I had no choice. But I'd never been robbed because I have that gift of gab. The guys back off if you don't show fear and charm them.

As I was about to pull out of the lot on this particular Thursday night, Arthur, the dispatcher, yelled to me that I had a call, an important call. At least that was what the person had said. I parked the cab near the gate, got out and walked across the lot to the office. The tune to a television commercial for a new hamburger offered at McDonald's tormented my mind. The dispatcher held the phone out to me and glanced at his watch. This call was eating into my drive time; it was on his dime. Money lost. I could smell the garlic from the late-dinner pizza on his breath.

"Hello?" I felt my scalp tingle.

"Mrs. Cutter? I can barely hear you. It seems we have a bad connection here."

"Who is this?" I didn't recognize the voice.

"This is Lyle Jeffreys, the private detective you hired to inquire about your ex. Remember now? Anyway, I'd like to meet with you after your shift. I'm waiting for one last call but I may have some good news

117

for you. If I don't hear from you, I'll come by tomorrow. There's no rush."

I refused to get my hopes up but I agreed to meet him. Numbed by the news of a possible breakthrough, I took the phone away from my ear and stared at it. Everything inside me seemed to fold in on itself. The private eye's words struck me like a physical blow to my heart, and I gasped for breath for a moment. I thought about taking Roger with me to meet this guy. He gave me the creeps but everyone said he was good at his job. Arthur saw the muddled expression on my face, touched my arm and asked me what was wrong.

"Nothing, just a crank call," I answered, ran to my cab and started my night. I didn't want everybody knowing my business.

My first fare was three young white guys, dressed in suits. Probably in their early twenties, in college or something. All of them were drunk, but one, a pale fella with long blond hair and freckles, was especially tanked. The others seemed to be consoling him, trying to keep him from getting hysterical. They didn't seemed to be doing a good job of it. He kept trying to jump out of the cab while it was moving in traffic.

"Herb, you agreed to marry her and it's too late to back out," one of his friends told him in a low voice. "Hey, you gave your word. My dad says you're not really a man until you get married and take a wife. Settle down. You're blowing it in school and plus you knocked her up, man, so you got to face the music. Game over, man, game over."

Herb kept whining and trying to get the door open. "She told me she couldn't get pregnant, told me I didn't need a condom. Marriage is a female plot to ruin men."

"Grow up, Herb," his other pal said. "You brought this on yourself. Let's get blotto and forget all about this junk. Life blows anyway." He ordered me to pull over at this trendy club down in Soho, and they paid, then staggered out, carrying their drunken friend with them.

The next fare was a young black couple in finely cut business suits, going somewhere after a long workday in the business district. They were talking about the worst dates they'd endured during their time on the mating market, the life of the lonely professional. I could tell them something about loneliness, for it took me three years before I could look at another man after my ex left.

"I was dumb to go along with it in the first place," the woman, tall, slender with the pulled-back hair, said. "A mutual friend set it up and the guy sounded like a million dollars on the phone. Told me all this baloney about how tall he was, how he looked, how much money he made. And he had the greatest voice. I was smart because I went to our meeting place, this little diner not far from my job, about ten minutes early and waited to check him out. What a frog! I didn't even introduce myself. I just split."

Both people laughed until they were holding their sides. "The only time I went on that kind of date, the woman showed up with four of her girlfriends," her friend, a banana-colored hunk with a friendly face, neatly trimmed goatee and closely cut black hair, said. "They took turns asking me questions, sizing me for their friend, who was absolutely perfect and a real looker. But I didn't bother with her because she came as a part of a package deal. Complete with her crew, and they were damn obnoxious."

"What do you have to do to find somebody decent in this town?" the woman asked with both amusement and alarm.

In a minute, her male friend put his arm around her and whispered something in her ear, and she giggled. She leaned back, resting her head on his arm, and lifted her face. I could tell he was getting excited because something in his voice changed when he said she was so terrific, so attractive and sweet that she deserved better, then he started kissing her. Deep, passionate kisses. And she let him.

I thought they were just friends but it seemed that they were much more. These two were natural exhibitionists, loved to be watched, to shock and titillate whomever was eyeballing them. Maybe they'd done this kind of thing before. The woman smiled wickedly as I adjusted the overhead mirror for a better view of their steamy antics, knowing that I would not intervene or look away. She winked once and closed her thin fingers around his dick, letting it stiffen in her grasp before she began milking him with long, even strokes. When he moaned too loud, she stifled him with a kiss, then proceeded to slide his unbuttoned pants over his knees. Her head disappeared into his lap, bobbing up occasionally while she licked and sucked his pole. Slurping and sucking

119

sounds filled the cab. All I could see was his face, sweating and pinched with ecstasy, tensing each time she descended upon him.

"Can you drive us up through Central Park?" he rasped, barely able to get out the words. "And take your time, please. There's a huge tip in it for you."

I nodded in agreement, turning off the Henry Hudson, that long stretch of road that runs along the western length of Manhattan to the Bronx and beyond toward Connecticut. Now and then I shot a glance at my side mirror to assure that no police cars were in the vicinity. That would be bad for all concerned.

The woman kept to her work, surfacing for air, then diving back onto his dick. I saw his massive hand cover the back of her head, slowly and gently, and eased her mouth over him once more. Meanwhile, I was getting hot as hell. I felt myself moisten between my legs, and it became really hard to focus on the traffic. One guy pulled alongside me, nodding toward the rear to alert me to the couple now fucking in the back seat with full abandon. The woman sat on top of her lover, straddling him with her legs as wide as they could go, bouncing on him in a demented rhythm borne of decadence and lust. Part of their excitement came not from his dick ramming into her with such hard intensity but from the knowledge I was watching them, completely entranced by their sexual boldness and totally aroused. A woman can sense when another woman has crossed the border into wanton desire, and I was definitely there. I couldn't wait to get home to Roger.

I unzipped my jeans, moved aside my soaked panties and plunged my fingers into myself. The woman was pressed back against the seat and partition so I felt every dip, every thrust, every grind of their brazen act. She cried out, her voice almost making the windows rattle, for him to hit it harder, faster, to make her cum again. Her hands sank into the firm flesh of his wide shoulders as he plowed into her with all his strength. Until she shouted his name to the choppy beat of his body arching up to get deeper inside her: "…Tommy…Tommy…Tommy." I saw the orgasm coming, building, gathering force inside her body like a hurricane gaining power out over the ocean, and she suddenly stopped, stiffened and shook before cradling her face in her hands. While she rained kisses on his nose and mouth, she purred like a contented cat.

"Thanks for the show," I cracked, causing both of them to chuckle. "Just pay the meter, no tip required. Have a nice night."

The couple jumped out of the cab on the other side of the park near Rockefeller Center, gave me a large tip anyway and walked off arm-in arm among the swirl of fallen yellow and brown leaves. I pulled off on a side street, leaned back on the seat and rubbed my dripping pussy until I was happily relieved.

The next fare was an older black man, his eyes distorted by horn-rimmed glasses with Coke-bottle lenses, carrying two shopping bags full of ancient 78 records. He paid me his fare as soon as he got in the cab. Gave me a five-dollar bill, said the fare cost the same every night. His mouth didn't stop running the entire ride. Nutty as a fruitcake and just as sweet in a way. Probably lonely as hell. Lot of lonely people in this big city.

"You see, I'm what they call a conspiracy buff, up on all of the government's evil doings," the old guy piped up. "The government's behind every dastardly deed you can imagine: They killed the Kennedy boys and Dr. King; they killed Marilyn Monroe because she knew too much; they never told you what really went on when they landed on the moon and found those alien life-forms; they don't tell you the truth about the black choppers that you see every now and then over the cities. Look at this global warming foolishness."

"And you probably believed they killed Elvis, right?" I joked.

"No, but they killed Sam Cooke, Jimi Hendrix and Marvin Gaye," he said, giving me a stern eye before jumping out of the cab at Times Square. "Don't laugh at things, young lady, you don't understand.'

I decided to go to a nearby diner for a midnight snack to kill some more time before I headed back out to the streets. Killing time, what a phrase.

For some reason, I suddenly flashed in my mind a picture of my hand clutching the solid muscle of Roger's dick, the thing twitching in my grasp, and feeling the urge to put it in my mouth. I laughed to myself when I really thought about this. For three years after my husband left, I'd sworn off men, just so I could heal and recover. There was a time when I could have had my pick of suitors when I was younger. After Benny, my ex, I never let a man get close enough to find out where I lived. I never expected to have another man in my life, let alone to be in love.

Most nights if I wanted to get off, I'd hold the detachable shower-head blasting full out between my legs, driving myself nearly nuts with each blast of warm water. And then came Roger, first into my life as a friend without any of the sex games. Never tried once to get me into bed. I made the first move. I could relax with him in the same way women only dream to be able to do with their men. Both lovers and friends. That perfect match. Often he'd drop by late at night just to talk or have a drink and never was there a hint that he desired me. It was just cool.

Four cups of black coffee and seven hours later, I parked the cab at the garage, signed out and called home. There was no answer. I thought all kinds of wicked thoughts while driving through the city to get to Harlem. I parked outside of our brownstone, making sure that the car was on the right side of the street to meet the city's traffic regulations and ran up the stairs. The apartment was in one piece, but there were a bunch of empty beer bottles on the kitchen table and several overflowing ashtrays. I looked into the bedroom where Roger was sprawled across the bed, asleep in his boxers, with his Johnson sticking straight up like a strong bit of pine.

Licking my lips, I remembered the first time I'd seen him without his clothes on after imagining all sorts of things about how he'd be hung, maybe hung like a horse. Or a bull. But his was a stubby thickness, almost as wide as his hand. That first time, he stripped in my living room, turned to face me real casual, gave me a smoldering gaze. The kind of look that made your panties bunch up. Even his deep, husky, mahogany voice set my juices flowing. He told me that he appreciated I was not the type of black woman who put her man down. But then he was not the type of man who saw himself as some kind of big swinging dick. He was human, very human, and considerate. That made all the difference in the world.

I crawled over to him, my lover in his slumber, and did like I had on many evenings when I found him this way. I started to jack him off, stroking him softly, using my other hand to arouse myself. I watched his closed eyes for any signs of activity, listened to the rhythms of his body, my radar on full alert. Then clutching his swollen shaft, I carefully stroked its length with such intense concentration that I thought he would awake startled. I didn't stop until his entire body shook, sending jets of hot seed onto his stomach and thighs. He never moaned or groaned. He was always silent, only his flesh revealed the depths of his ecstasy. Once he had climaxed, I realized that I wanted more so I climbed atop him, stabbing myself with his bit of solid pine. I touched my clit as I grinded myself on him, moving from side to side. Thrusting and bobbing on his dick, I found myself cumming so much that I didn't feel that he was shooting inside me at the same time. It was so good, much too good. Here I was past my prime, with a real man in my life, happy that I had someone who accepted me for who I was, someone who didn't label me as oversexed because I enjoyed making love. I wanted more loving, although I had collapsed on top of his strong, male body. My head felt light, and spots of various colors appeared suddenly before my eyes but I said nothing when he took me and entered me again slowly from behind. Then he lubricated himself with our combined juices and made love to me in the one place where I had never been penetrated. He rode harder and deeper until the room started tilting. and I came like I'd never done before.

Afterward, cradling his head under his linked fingers, he laid on his back and spoke quietly to me. "Once I lost a woman I truly, truly loved by trying to possess her, by trying to own her. I won't make that same mistake with you."

"Are you really mine?" I asked, resting on my stomach next to him.

"Yes, all yours." He touched my shoulder with a gentle stroke of his hand and played with the hair on the back of my neck.

"I love being with you," I told him, my eyes full of adoration and longing. I sat beside him on the bed, examining the wet spots where our bodies had lain, and wiped the small beads of sweat from his furrowed forehead with a folded pillowcase. My hand brushed along his damp groin against something that craved further attention. I closed my eyes and fell upon him with a hungry mouth and a deep sigh. The coffee would have to wait and so would my call to the private detective. Old debts didn't matter at a time like this. Pure bliss. You know what I mean, don't you, ladies? Everything can wait. Just a little while longer.

I REMEMBER YOU

Kenny was driving crazy, like he was late for work. Which he was. He ran two red lights, almost ran a car off the road and nearly side swiped another one. A police siren was the last thing he wanted to hear on this morning. His boss at the plant, a big Russian guy with a heavy accent and the constant smell of vodka on his breath, told him yesterday if he was late anymore not to bother coming to work. His alarm clock failed once again and here he was trying to make up time by taking shortcuts to the highway. And now the cops.

He thought about making a run for it since the highway was only three blocks away. But the last thing he needed was a trumped-up charge of fleeing the cops and a possible stay behind bars. The police car snagged him at the next light, its driver motioning frantically for him to pull over. He did as he was told and parked the car. The cop stopped quickly behind him and jumped out of the car with ticket book in hand.

"Hello officer. I didn't see that light back there," Kenny said quickly, setting up the foundation for a tempest of lies he hoped would con the cop into letting him off with a warning. "I really didn't see the light. I'm late for work, and I just wasn't thinking. I'm very sorry."

The cop, who he could see was a woman, was dressed in the usual uniform, but her wide sunglasses shielded her face from view. "Good morning, sir. Let me see your license and registration."

Kenny, frowning, handed over the documents and started up with the excuses again. "See, it's like this. I've got this bastard of a boss who told me if I didn't get there on time, he'd fire me. I can't let that happen. I have all kinds of bills. I can't afford to lose this job. Can't you show a little mercy? My life's hanging in the balance here. Please, officer."

"No way, sir," the officer said sternly. "Can you get out of the vehicle, please?" She placed her hand on her holster and stepped back so he could get out.

With him standing against his car, she reviewed his documents, making a note on her pad. "Is this your real name?"

"Yes, officer, Kenny Davis." He said it proudly.

The cop lifted her glasses, scowled and moved closer so she could see her face. Her hand never left her gun. She enjoyed the fact that he was terrified of her, nearly wetting his pants from the anxiety. "Do you recognize me, Mr. Davis?"

Cars slowed to see what was going on with the cop and the detained driver, rubbernecking out of curiosity. She impatiently waved them on and stepped even closer to the man. He thought her face looked familiar, someone he knew from the old days, but he couldn't place her. Who was she? The name was right on the tip of his tongue.

"I remember you, yeah," he suddenly shouted. "Pamela...Pamela Newton."

She flicked her glasses back into place. "Right, Pamela Newton. Pamela, the girl you stood up on prom night and never called. The girl you dissed. The girl you played for a fool."

He started shuffling his feet, thinking about running. "Hey, that was a long time ago. I was a young punk, didn't know nothing from nothing. I didn't mean to hurt you or nothing. I didn't mean any harm. I just got tied up. Really, I'm sorry about that."

"I'm sorry, too, Mr. Davis," she sneered. "You have no idea how much pain you caused me. How stupid I felt sitting there all night, waiting for you to call. Crying my eyes out. Totally crushed by an insensitive ass like you. Yes, you're sorry alright."

"But that was years ago," he pleaded. "That has nothing to do with this ticket."

The cop was still angry, just the memory of his mistreatment of her

125

stirred up old feelings of resentment and hate. "No, it has everything to do with this ticket."

"What are you going to do?" he asked, looking at her regretfully.

"You know what, get in your car and follow me. We have an old debt to settle. Today is the day I collect. If you even think about making a run for it, I'll get on the horn and tell the dispatcher that you took a shot at me and then every cop in the county will be gunning for you. So if I were you, I'd do as I was told."

He nodded passively, still thinking about that prom night and how payback can be a real bitch. "Sure, officer."

He got in his car and followed the police car out on the highway, out past the neatly lined suburban homes, past the big oil refinery tanks and on to the straight stretch of interstate heading nowhere. They drove for what seemed like hours until she turned into a roadside rest stop and parked. He didn't know what to think, maybe she was going to shoot him. What was the saying about a woman scorned?

She exited her car and walked over to him. "Mr. Davis, don't even think about running. I don't want this to get out of hand."

He followed her to a small roadside building, which was often used by truckers and motorists to revive after a long drive. The brick structure had a few windows, each covered by wire mesh, and two wooden benches inside, as well as an old couch. Vending machines offering soft drinks, bottled juices, potato chips, cookies and other snacks lined one wall. Other than that, the place smelled musty, oily and was deserted.

"What are you going to do to me?" he asked, backing away.

"Something I wanted to do a long time ago," she said curtly. "You hurt me real bad. Do you know that?"

"Yes, I do. I'm sorry. Really sorry."

"I was crazy in love with you," she said, locking the door from the inside. Bolting it. "And you broke my heart. Do you know how many times I dreamed of this moment?"

"No." He answered her, but his mind was on escape. There was no back door.

Slowly, she removed her gun belt and laid it on the bench near her. The gun was all he saw, the gun that could cause him pain and injury. He thought about falling on his knees, begging her for forgiveness. But then he knew that pitiful act wouldn't work with her. She wanted something, maybe blood. Maybe his blood.

"Take off your clothes, Mr. Davis," she ordered. "Every stitch."

"You've got to be kidding, right," he asked, his eyes almost tearing.

"No, I'm not," she replied, moving toward her gun belt.

"Come on, that was a long time ago. You can't fault me for something I did as a kid."

"I can, and I will," she said, watching him hopping with one leg still stuck in his trousers. "Hurry, Mr. Davis, I don't have all day. Let's get this over with."

He stood before her naked, ashamed and terrified, holding his hands over his privates. "I love a girl in uniform, always gets me hot and bothered," he joked but stopped short of laughing when he saw the serious look on her face.

"On your knees before me, here, right here!" She pointed to a spot inches in front of her, clenching her teeth. "Do it now!"

She was a fine black woman, quite attractive. About thirty. His age. He really couldn't remember why he stood her up back then on prom night, left her sitting in her expensive, custom-made dress in her living room while he hung out with the boys, drinking and raising hell. She had every right to be pissed, but to keep a grudge this long was nuts. Her voice barked at him again, ordering him to kneel and close his eyes. He obeyed without any back talk. His ears picked up the sounds of her removing her own clothes, the thud of shoes falling and the swoosh of satin panties sliding over smooth, brown thighs.

"Open your eyes and come here," she said in a darker voice. "Snap to it!"

He opened his eyes and saw her, standing with one bare leg propped on one of the benches. Her gun was still within reach. She kept her blue regulation police blouse on, with its shield and insignia, but there was nothing concealing the plump mocha-colored lips of her box from view, except a few tufts of black pubic hair. He knew what she wanted now. What he had denied her that night so many years ago.

"You won't cheat me again," she snapped. "I was a virgin. I was saving it for you. You were supposed to be my first, and you cheated me. But no more!"

On his hands and knees, he crawled to the tasty cherry opening, exposing the slit even more by parting her thighs with a push of his hands. A shudder of delight went through her as he probed for its prize with his mouth, lapping around its pronounced folds with quick, sharp moves of his tongue. He felt her sag a little when he rimmed her opening carefully, finally slipping his stiff pink tongue into the very depths of her. Her legs quivered. The desire to be filled, to be sexed, to be loved grew within her with each penetration of his tongue, and her hands held his head steady while she felt wave upon wave of orgasmic fire engulf her loins.

"Kenny, oh Kenny, I knew it would be like this," she moaned. "It's so good, baby. Don't deny me now. Take it all, Kenny."

As he ran his tongue along the opening of her hole and into the saucy interior, he tasted the sweetness of her fluids, catching the unending flow that now seeped onto his lips and chin. She chanted that she felt so close to him, so much a part of him, that he'd never been far from her mind. Much of what she said was lost in the heavy, choppy breaths that swallowed her words. They wasted no time getting it on. Soon, she was riding him wildly, grinding her clit against the base of his crotch, cramming his tool deeper into her tunnel. They went at it harder and faster, his dick warring with her clenching inner muscles.

"It's incredible, Kenny. All these years, all these years," she panted. "So long, so long, I waited so long. Give it to me, darling. Fill me up, fill me up."

He dived as far as he could into her, occasionally rubbing her G-spot on the down stroke, sending flashes of unending sensation through her lower body. It was her dream come true, them together. She wrapped one leg around his middle to give him an even deeper angle of entry, farther into the tightness of her sex. Her shivers and groans alerted him to the fact that she was close to another burst, another climax, another peak from the most carnal of rhythms. Coupling. Their bodies slammed together violently, sending off a thunderous sound that rocked the room. He refused to lose his seed too soon. He wanted her to remember this day as she had that other horrible one years ago. Although she was beyond wet, he held her butt up so he would remain hard and firm within her on each thrust, but suddenly her muscles contracted in a death grip around him as the first spasms of her most profound orgasm struck without warning. She suddenly sat up, clutched him to her, kissing him more passionately then ever. Her eyes were fixed on his face when it hit the last and strongest time, and she felt joy, compassion and tenderness for this man she'd hated for so long. Too long.

"Oh Kenny...Kenny." She laughed when it was all over, her arms around his neck, her lips nestled securely against his bare chest.

"What about my job?" he wailed. "I'm screwed."

She kissed his throat, the place where a pulse still pounded, before squeezing him against her. "Don't worry, love. I'll help you get something you won't mind going to every day."

They looked at each other and grinned. Both still reeling from the storm of their lovemaking in the tiny locked room.

"Is there a chance for us now, Kenny?" she asked, her voice hopeful.

"I don't see why not," he replied, looking for his shirt. "You're the best thing to happen in my life in quite some time. I don't figure to mess it up like before. You can bank on that."

FEMALE TROUBLE

7.11.2001

113 rue du Faubaurg Poissonniere
Paris, France 75009

Dearest Jean:

   First, let me tell you that I'm alright, that I got the money you sent me. And, yes, I'm still working at the little bookstore on the Left Bank, and they're treating me very good. Armand's. I wanted to get a job as a salesclerk at the famed Shakespeare & Co. on 12 rue de L'Odeon over in the same area, where Ernest Hemingway used to hang out, but they weren't hiring. They say James Baldwin used to go there too. This is only the second letter I've written you in the three months I've been here in Gay Paree. What a city! The City of Lights! Thank you for being a real friend.

   For the first few weeks, I did the tourist thing, walking along the rows of chestnut trees lining the Champs Elysee, gawking at the Arc de Triomphe, riding the Metro, visiting the Louvre (an exquisite art museum), touring the narrow streets of Montmartre and Clichy where Henry Miller (he's a writer; wrote nasty books) ran around. Saw the Cathedral of Notre Dame and waited for the hunchback to swing down and take me away. Watched the lovers cuddle and smooch along the Seine. God, I'm so glad I came here.

As you know, Pops never wanted me to leave home. He couldn't believe that Bing's little girl would do something like this. Leave home and go across the water to some foreign city and live. When I first left, he sent me this ten-page letter, reminding me what being a good girl meant. How I must not lose my values or virtue. How important it was to remember what being a lady means. There was all of this junk in the letter about how hard times were in the sixties when you two first married and how faith and values brought you guys through it all. Then he launched into all of this stuff about the sanctity of marriage, filthy sex in everything in society, in the movies, ads, and even television. "Give the idea of remaining chaste until marriage some real thought," he wrote, "because you could otherwise fall into a sordid life of promiscuity, getting diseases or an unwanted baby." He said marriage is not only a sacrament of the church but a "binding contract entered by two persons who willingly agree to forge a life together."

Then there was this whole part about how marriage isn't easy. How it means sticking together when times are tough. How it means sticking together when one of the people gets sick, loses a job or gets on your nerve. He also said that he wrote the letter because he couldn't stand the thought of me living with a guy before getting married. The fact that Didier, whom everybody calls Knowledge, was married once before and has a kid especially irks him. And I think he also doesn't like that Didi (my pet name for him) is from Tunisia, part-Arab, a real African-American. Didi's father is from Mississippi, the Delta. Was here in the service in Paris on leave and met Didi's mom. So Pops said if Didi left the woman he married and his kid, then he'll really mess me over. That's wack.

Also, he said Didi is not in my class, a foreigner, an alien. Said he doesn't want to see me hurt. Said I could do better. Said he couldn't see how our "entanglement" could end up any way but in grief and heartache. Said he knew how hard it is for a young girl to start a life but I should think about his offer to send me to Harvard or Columbia. Asked me to not throw my life away with this "camel jockey." God, that kind of talk about my lover hurt. Ordered me to make up my mind by August so I can be in school by fall. Then he closed it all with how he loved me very much and only wanted to see me happy. Now you can see why I haven't written, Jean. So much on my mind.

Believe me, I know I'll never be the most famous woman on the planet, but I do want to leave my mark on it. I want people to know I was here. That's probably youth talking, huh? Jean, before I go on with this letter, you should know that I don't want you to let anyone read this. You know how my pops gets if he finds out about anything about me and the real world. He's always been too protective of me, even when I was small. His Little Princess. I recall you telling me just before I split there that Pops loved me too much, adored me, but I can't deal with that thing. It's too stifling, too oppressive.

And his saying that he loves me, well, that means nada to me because he's never acted like he did. I remember how he acted when I got my period for the first time, how he used to monitor my phone calls, how he used to shadow me in his damn Bonneville, how he acted when I got little bee-stung breasts, how he acted when I came home with my first hickey after my first concert. He bugged out each time and acted like I was a slut. I had to get away before he smothered me to death with his love.

All I remember him saying is: "I should have had boys. Females ain't nothing but trouble and every man knows that there ain't nothing worse than female trouble." I don't think he ever knew how little and insignificant that remark made me feel. Like I was nothing. I remember he got mad at me because I slipped up and said *fuck*. Didn't talk to me for six months. That almost killed me.

However, Jean, you were always another story. Unlike my parents, you always told me I could do anything I wanted to do. When I was sixteen and dating that twenty-year-old Nigerian drummer, you took it in stride because you knew I wouldn't let him get to first base. He wasn't getting no nookie, and you knew it because you knew me inside. You said it was no big thing about me wearing black clothes and sunglasses, piercing my tongue, listening to hardcore rap and hanging out in the downtown clubs. You listened to me when I got hurt after having a crush on some stupid boy and never judged me, not once. You let

132

me cry on your shoulder until the hurt went away. Mom kept saying over and over that she warned me about boy,s but you let me be myself like a true friend. For all of this, I love you, Jean, more than words could ever say.

Jean, the real reason I'm writing is to ask you about sex and love. I think this is my first real love. Do you remember how it was for you when you were in love for the first time? I think it does something to your mind as well as your body. What a special feeling! It can't possibly last. It's so strong, so powerful, so total. Didi says he feels it too. He teases me because I'm so petite, five-four, but he says I have a great body. Jean, we went for a walk along the bookstalls on the quay one night, and he kissed me, our first kiss, on the Pont Neuf bridge. It was strictly high-voltage. Do you remember your first real kiss? Does it ever get that good again?

Now for the X-rated part, don't read any further if you don't want to know the real nitty-gritty, but I felt I had to tell you everything. I told you when I made love for the first time back there, the pain, my embarrassment at bleeding and the unexplained reason why I wanted to do it again so fast afterward. I was scared when the guy started kissing and feeling me up because I knew it was going to happen, that this was going to be The Night. Scared that I'd tear down there and bleed and never stop bleeding. So scared but hot and wanting him. I was eighteen. You asked if he used protection and said it was all a part of becoming a woman. You were so understanding and modern. But now there is Didi. Didi and his sculptured Arab face. He is such a good lover, so patient, so skillful. He taught me how to take all of him in me, how to give him love back. (I can see you frowning now.) Sometimes when I leave him to go to work, I see flashes of erotic images in my head like he is still inside me, still with me physically as well as spiritually. The way he puts his finger under my chin and gazes soulfully into my eyes. His hand resting gently in the small of my naked back. His feather-soft kisses in the sensitive crook of my legs. The sexual heat radiating in waves of almost visible rays from his wiry tan body. The tip of his tongue in my ear. His teeth nibbling at my earlobe. My lips swollen and puffy from hours and hours of kisses. The lustful gleam in his black eyes while he watches me model silk teddies for him. He likes garter belts and stockings too. The feeling of my oiled skin in a see-through lace body-suit. The sizzle of our sex talk until well after midnight. His fingers in the silky crotch of my panties, his hot breath on my nipples, my fingers curled around his hot cock. Jean, I finally know what it feels like to be a woman at twenty-three. Remember what it was like for you when you were my age.

I know you don't want to get a blow-by-blow of it all. Jean, he only thought of my pleasure, of my ecstasy. All my nervousness left my body at the moment of his gentle touch. That hunger, that desire that I once feared, flared up with his kisses and caresses, then faded to a low, constant hum, but it awakened as our bodies wrapped around each other, taking on new shapes. Sometimes he'd pause from warming my body with his hands and mouth and just admire me, worship me until the spell of the moment would be broken. Oh, love is so incredible! He could have taken me then and there, but he did not. Instead, he built the flame in me into mounting waves of burning emotion. You know what I mean, into a peak for which I have no words. Incredible, really! While he would fondle every part of me, I could feel the hunger come back, sweeping over my skin, inch by inch, nerve by nerve. I feel like I was reborn, like a new being. We'd get worked up into such a state of desire, of hunger that we couldn't wait to possess each other. Then he moved so we danced together on the bed, our bodies joined at the front, at the heart, so we could see everything and feel everything. He told me that he was so hard that it hurt.

After he touched me there, he said he could feel the heat coming from me while he explored me with a finger. He got up on his knees and put his erection at the opening of my sex and teased me with it until I could barely catch a breath. Once he entered me, he held me by the waist to control how deeply his strokes would be and proceeded to slam me back against him. He never went all the way inside at first, choosing to pull out and rub himself against my hole. Listening to my short gasps, he stopped completely inside me, letting me feel him stiffen until he was like a rod of metal. I could feel myself contracting and tightening around him as he started pumping inside my body before exploding inside my vault, shooting jets of juice deep into me, after a few short, hard thrusts. We soared together. When Didi finished, he leaned back

134

against the wall, his limp dick sliding out to rest against his muscular thigh. I gave him a little time to relax before I got underneath him and placed him into my mouth to suck him back into readiness. As I pumped my hand along his shaft, never moving my lips from the head of his dick, I closed my eyes and felt his rapid heartbeat through the swollen veins of his hardened flesh. His hips shimmied a little when I took the entire length of him deep into my throat, sucking him hard, especially along the puffed head of his dick. He was murmuring about how he was going to cum again and built the rhythm of my bobbing head with a full intensity designed to leave him totally pleasured. Suddenly, he came, all over my sensitive breasts, twitching, his body writhing above me, all covered with sweat. I imagine what we will do once he recovers from this. Start all over again. I can't get enough of him. Is that bad? Didi is the first man to show me how to experience something deeper in love, something almost sacred. How can you describe feelings that take you out of your body? What words can explain what it really feels like to have a man embedded in your deepest parts, making you scream, making you speak in tongues? How many men and women have felt like this, I wonder?

So far, I've only had sex with three guys, including Didi. Some girls sleep with as many guys as they can, get knocked up as Pops calls it, or have four or five abortions before they're even twenty. And by the time they're in their forties, they're all messed up down there, worn out. Not me, Jean. As someone said, my body is my temple, and I respect that.

Jean, help me with this. I need to address something that Pops said in his letter about Didi being "not in my class." Whatever. Didi is studying to be a chef at The Sorbonne—cooking pastries and meats his specialty—so my father has nothing to worry about in that regard. This is not Life 101. Didi is a good man. He says he's only half a soul without me. Isn't that sweet? He works part-time as a drummer with this jazz combo over at a club in Montmartre, which is not too far from our little apartment in Pigalle. When I met him, he had three roommates, a fuzzy-haired art student, a nutty stand-up comic, and this big, buxom stripper named Chantal. I made him throw them out. We live the perfect Boho life, the real Dada life, drinking espresso and pernod, hanging out with the Arabs and Africans at La Grande Halles, going to all of the cafes like Tiptop, Marcel's, Meow-Meow, Le Fleur, Von's and Bonbons. I love him, and I love it here.

From Didi, I've learned about love, mature love, real love. About selflessness, oneness, faith and commitment. About tenderness and intimacy. About trusting love and its healing power. I know now that truth brings people closer together. With love, once you get past the sex, you soon learn the real deal about people. I hope I haven't shocked you with this letter, Jean. I haven't become a sex freak. I'm just a young woman in love, trying to understand what it all means. As I look out my window, I'm mesmerized by the postcard view over the roofs of Paris east to the Eiffel Tower in the distance. I can't come home now. Tell my parents that for me. I'm going to stay here and give love a chance. Well, I'm going to take a catnap before I go to work. I love you madly.

Sincerely,
Denise

P.S. Jean, we're careful. We've pledged to remain faithful so there is no need to be anxious about anything. Also, don't forget to burn this letter after you read it. Oh yes, my phone number here is 011-321-84366835. Call after six at night.

THE UNUSED BED

D r. Brenda Gooding could not sleep. She tossed and turned her lanky, athletic, dark frame in her bed, lying first on her stomach and then on her side. Another trick of burying her head under the covers and pillows didn't work either, so she got up and walked to the living room. A glance at the wall clock revealed that it was only three in the morning. She should have been asleep hours ago but her mind was fully alert although her body was bone-tired. Her husband, also a doctor, was out of town at a convention in Denver, giving a paper on the new line of cancer-fighting drugs coming to market after three years of human trials. The drugs, synthetically produced, starved the blood supply of growing tumors, causing most of them to wither and die. Those that were stubborn could be fought, with some success, with a battery of chemotherapy and radiation.

However, she was a psychiatrist and author of the bestselling book, *The Flow Of Love: Becoming An Multi-Orgasmic Couple,* specializing in female sexual problems in a marital setting. Along with her office hours, she met with a group of women who gathered every Friday to discuss their sexual difficulties in an old converted warehouse downtown. There were ten women in the group, hailing from all types of careers and economic backgrounds. This current mix of personalities, she thought, made for lively, very candid sessions frequently, with the women urging to go even deeper into their feelings about the barrier to full, complete intimacy with their husbands.

She stood at the window, watching the moon shine luminously down on the hill where their bungalow held down a corner of the tree-lined street that ran to the shoreline. Once she poured the drink, vodka straight, she settled on the sofa and let the burning alcohol course through her body, lulling her closer to a false sense of relaxation. Nothing about a vodka-induced slumber appealed to her but she had little choice because tomorrow, or rather today, promised to be extremely difficult. There were meetings in the morning with administrators about a satellite clinic to be opened in one of the more disadvantaged neighborhoods in the inner city, tons of paperwork to be filled out, lunch with two old friends who were trying to convince her to work with them on a proposal for federal funding for a research project and then later the patient sessions. After two stiff drinks, she finally fell asleep on the sofa, curled up in a fetal position.

At the group session later, Dr. Gooding sat in her chair at the head of the table, looking benignly at the women gathered before her and the two large pitchers of iced tea. All black women, all accomplished in some way. All troubled by crumbling marriages with major problems that could be traced back to the bedroom. She surveyed them as they sat attentively waiting for her to kick things off.

"So many times I've said that good sex starts outside the bedroom," the doctor started in a calm voice. "If there are problems in how you relate and communicate in other areas in your marriage, those difficulties will find their way into your sex life. Fortunately, if you want to save your marriages, you must approach them head-on by finding new ways to recharge your love life, to change the negative patterns that are robbing your relationships of their vitality and joy. You don't have to accept the way things are, you can move forward if you make your marriage a priority."

Pauline, a thirty-eight-year-old banker, raised her hand, waving it eagerly. "Doctor, Doctor, I want to finish what I was saying at our last session. There have been some new developments at home, and I want to share them with the group, if I could."

"Go ahead, tell us what's up," Dr. Gooding replied after taking a poll of the expressions on the other women's faces. They didn't seem to mind Pauline going first.

"As you know, my husband and I haven't had sex in quite a while," Pauline said sadly. "It used to be great with us. We had sex every day, twice even three times sometimes. Now we're lucky if we have it once every four or five months. That's killing me because I'm very sexual, and I want to jump him every time I see him but I hold back. And he often doesn't approach me. I think he avoids me because he doesn't believe he satisfies me. He does. We both use sex for different reasons, my husband to show me that he cares and me to show him who's the boss. It's the only place where I feel I have control. He runs every other aspect of our house, and I have very little say."

"How many other women here have a similar problem?" The doctor asked for a show of hands and three others waved theirs enthusiastically.

"We stopped having sex two years after our honeymoon when we found out that we couldn't conceive a child," Janet, a buyer for a department chain, blurted out in a loud voice. She usually talked in a near shout as if she were afraid no one would notice her. "I don't see the reason to have sex if you can't make a baby. Sex is the last thing on my mind. He goes out and does his thing. I don't care as long as the bills get paid. And I have my vibrator, dildos and other toys, so I'm content."

Everyone laughed but Dr. Gooding, who kept a stern look in her eyes, and asked once more if there was anyone else who faced the same dilemma as Pauline. She glanced around the table for a moment until finally Natalie, a very shy, young bi-racial woman beautiful enough to be a model, spoke quietly with a hand over her mouth. Her husband was a batterer, a three-time offender, now back in the home for the first time in a year and a half following a stint in jail.

"You girls know how Wally is," Natalie, whose dark lovely looks frequently brought male stares on the street, said calmly. "He's always criticizing me about something. In his mind, there is a right and wrong way to do everything so everything I do gets reviewed. He's the perfect one and can't accept that someone else might have a point of view. He never talks to me like a human being, an equal, but more like a child. When we do talk, either he's sarcastic, angry and loud, putting me down, or sulking and not talking at all. He's really neat, well-organized and efficient, so he gets mad at me if I get sloppy sometimes or forget some"

"What does he do for a living?" Dr. Gooding asked. "And how is the sex?"

"He's a production manager at a high-tech firm and yes, the sex was really good but it was strange because he controlled everything—when and how we would have it," Natalie said, looking down at the table. "His favorite game was to have me dress like a young schoolgirl, everything white and virginal, and then we'd pretend he was a stranger who'd lured me back to his house after school. I know it sounds sick but I really got into it for a while, and he'd get so big and hard. I'd sit on his lap and French-kiss him all over while he fingered me. Then he'd sit back in the chair, and I'd straddle him, riding him slow, then fast suddenly like he liked it, with my hips rotating as I moved up and down on him. Once we got into it, I'd lean forward and grab the back of the chair for support, with him licking and sucking my breasts, talking to me: 'Tell your uncle Mark you love it, tell him he's all you need, tell him nobody could make you feel like this.' I climaxed with him like I'd never done with any man before. I don't feel good about a lot of the games we played but now he says I'm older, and he needs new thrills. He's been talking about tying me up, spanking and going to these sex clubs where there's all these leather, masks, whips and stuff. That's not me but I love him."

"Sick bastard," Portia, an independent bookseller with a husband with impotence woes, snarled. "Leave him, girl. Damn perv."

Dr. Gooding stood and walked to a cabinet across the room, pulled out a tray of pastry and cookies. Smiling, she walked back to the table, set down the tray and looked again at Pauline. "Pauline, you were talking about the problem of avoidance in your sex life with your husband. Continue, please."

While the other women helped themselves to the pastry and iced tea on the table, Pauline reached into her purse, pulled out a mint and popped it into her unpainted mouth. "My husband is an odd man. He always seems to forget things, and when I remind him, then he gets mad and stays mad. He never does what he promises to do. I have to stay on him to get anything done. I hate doing that because I feel like I'm his mother or something. He never accepts responsibility for anything he does; in fact it's always someone else's fault. He always turns things around so it looks like he's the victim. He's basically a nice person but he doesn't understand how his actions affect me. He never takes my feelings into account."

"Back to the sex, how is it when you do have it?" the doctor asked solemnly.

"He doesn't like to kiss, cuddle or hold me when we're having sex," Pauline said. "He likes to do the missionary position, with my legs up, so he can go deeper into me. He's a pretty nice size, above average, so he's not used to having to work during sex. He'll pound into me for more than a hour and a half, going real hard and fast, not once showing any tenderness or affection. Then he gets mad when I don't cum. I don't think I've ever come from actual intercourse, and he won't eat me down there. He's selfish when it comes to giving me pleasure. But he does other things, like we masturbate each other, talk about our fantasies, use toys on each other. Still, I feel so empty, so unfulfilled, so needy. Often after we finish making love, I'll go into the bathroom. Sit on the toilet, touch myself until I cum and cry."

"Get yourself a lover, sista, and find your own joy," Angela interrupted. Many of the other women clapped, shouted things in support, and urged the neglected woman to flee.

"That's not always the answer, not if you love the man and want to save the marriage," Dr. Gooding said. "Pauline, do you love him? Do you think your marriage is worth saving?"

"Yes, I love him, but I don't know how much more of this I can take," Pauline replied, her voice cracking. Janet, who was sitting next to her, reached over and held one of her trembling hands in a show of sisterhood.

Understanding that Pauline had reached her emotional limit for the session, Dr. Gooding switched her attention to Nancy, a twenty-nine-year-old housewife and cofounder of a neighborhood literacy program. She was like many women, who had suddenly buried themselves in motherhood and family at the expense of their femininity and appearance. In her case, she was married to a well-known corporate attorney, who traveled extensively on complex, controversial cases, often leaving the maintenance of the home to her.

"Elliott is much older than I am, in his mid-forties, and very accomplished," Nancy began in a firm voice. "I'm lucky to have such a powerful, handsome man in my life. He travels a great deal with his business, often leaving on Thursday and not getting back until the following Tuesday. Sometimes we go to these formal events at his job or out on the town or get together with other couples. Elliott is six-six, powerfully built, works out, and the women flock to him. And he's a flirt. Loves the attention. I knew that when I met him. At first, it was cute, the flirting made me feel special, but now it really bothers me. I'm pretty tied down with the kids—we have three—and most of the time I feel trapped. I'm at home while he's out in the world, having a real life."

"What about the sex?" the doctor asked, watching Portia chewing a cookie vigorously.

"When we have sex, it's physically satisfying but there isn't enough of it," Nancy groaned, tears welling in her eyes. "At first, I tried to punish him by saying I was having my period, had a headache, was upset about something, but I didn't like denying myself.

"One night I told him that I wanted everything, romance as well as the sex. More push-push in the bush. But that didn't do anything. He just told me that I was living in luxury, that most women would die to get the set-up I had, and hired a maid to help me around the house. Then he started traveling even more, and I'd never see him. I took a couple of lovers but they weren't my husband. I miss him in bed. My children, all three boys, look just like Elliott. One lover, a newspaper reporter, was really nice. He wanted me to leave Elliott, me and the kids, but I couldn't do that to the boys. So I had to cut that off."

"Why can't you leave?" Dr. Gooding asked. "Is there any love left in the relationship?"

Nancy's face turned to stone, her voice was firm and unwavering. "No, there's nothing left, but Elliott loves his boys, and I can't do that to him. I'm trapped, and there's no way out."

"We're all trapped, no way out...no way out!" Pauline wailed, bursting into tears. She looked hysterically at the other women seated at the table, sprang to her feet and ran wildly from the room. Everybody stood in shock but the doctor patiently asked them to sit down.

"Natalie, can you continue the discussion for the final ten minutes of the session?" Dr. Gooding asked as she strode toward the rear of the room where Pauline had locked herself in the bathroom. "Maybe you can talk about the dynamics of initiative, change and the twelve keys to sexual empowerment, the topics of last session."

The doctor put her ear to the large wooden door, listening for any sounds that might indicate that Pauline could be harming herself, but all she heard was the endless rush of sighs and sobbing. As long as the woman was crying, she concluded, there was time to coax her from her new sanctuary, comforting words to soothe her inner pain, and quench her need for solitude and self-pity. She let minutes pass as Pauline cried until the suffering started to subside. The women finished the session behind her, said their good-byes and scurried to the exit. Now they were alone, one on one, and the real negotiations could begin in earnest.

"Pauline, can you hear me?" The doctor's voice was light as a gentle sea breeze, not a hint of alarm in it. "Pauline, answer me. Are you alright?"

The woman on the other side of the door sounded helpless, confused and desperate. "I'm sorry, Dr. Gooding, I didn't mean to act like that. I don't usually do that kind of thing. It felt like I was going to explode if I didn't get out of there. I'm so ashamed. I'm sorry, so sorry."

"Pauline, we all have our moments of weakness and pain," the doctor said, sounding much like a veteran hostage negotiator. "We've all been through what you're going through, including me. That's why we're all in this room, trying to become whole and strong again. I know it's been tough for you."

Again the sobbing started, building in pitch and intensity. "I'm such a fool. Such a fool. The other women must think I'm so stupid. How can I ever look them in the face again?"

"Nobody will hold what happen here today against you. If anything, it just shows that you have deep emotions, that the pain has not deadened your feelings. And Pauline, that's a very good thing, believe me. They're all gone. It's only you and me here now. If you won't come out, can I come in? We can talk until you feel better. No pressure, I promise."

A few anxious seconds passed, then the lock on the door sounded with an abrupt click, and it swung open. The women looked into each other's eyes, not a word uttered. In the doctor's analytical glance, she saw this pretty young thing who was tormented and terribly tempting since the first day they met. Pauline. Just the sight of Pauline in motion was enough to get her wet. When she came into the office that first day, she knew this woman had never been properly kissed, caressed or loved. All of Pauline's true sexual desires were suppressed, dormant.

"Come on out, Pauline, the others are gone," Dr. Gooding said, holding out her hand. "We're alone."

Passively, Pauline followed the doctor out into the larger room, into the fading sunlight.

"Do you mind if I ask you a direct question, Pauline?"

"Go ahead," Pauline said, giving the doctor a sweet smile.

The older woman, still strikingly beautiful, walked over to her client, sensing the potential for erotic possibilities in the air, and placed her dark-chocolate face close to that of the emotionally unsteady woman. She filled her nostrils with the woman's jasmine scent, softly whispering she could ease her pain, in an almost singsong way. With a graceful motion, she lightly brushed the side of Pauline's downy face with her fingertips.

"Pauline, let me take care of you, let me heal you," the doctor said soothingly. "Give yourself to me. I promise I won't hurt you. I really can give you some clarity and peace of mind. Trust me."

"What's your question?" Her client pulled back and searched the older woman's face with a quick gaze. "What do you want to know?"

"Pauline, have you ever been curious about what it would be like to have sex with a woman?" Dr. Gooding asked. "Ever? Ever wonder how it would be skin to skin with someone who feels what you feel, who knows just where to touch you, who knows how to hit all of your hot buttons. Only a woman truly knows what satisfies another woman."

"Well...I wondered what women did in bed together. What they did with all of the toys I, see them with. Of course, I've seen my husband's pornos, men seem to like watching women together. Men always talk about threesomes. But yes, watching women together, making love to each other so gently, so tenderly. The tenderness, I guess, that's what fascinates me about women being together. Men lack that."

"Not all men, Pauline. Some men can be quite tender...and bold."

The doctor sat at the long table, opened her purse and pulled out her silver cigarette case.

Pauline sat as well, watching the doctor with swollen, red-lidded eyes. "Can I have one of your cigarettes? Brenda, can I call you that?"

"Yes, take one from the pack. What''s on your mind? You're looking at me like you have something to ask." The doctor thought for a second about putting on her new Dee Dee Bridgewater CD, the *Live in Paris* one, but decided against it.

"Aren't you married, Brenda?" Pauline asked only the first part of her question but Dr. Gooding was trained in unearthing the unspoken, the implied, the inferred.

The doctor didn't hesitate, holding up her ring finger. "Yes, I'm married to a wonderful man, a doctor like myself. My husband understands me, knows me better than any other human being in this world. We have a very close, intimate bond that rarely involves sex, and although I have family and close girlfriends, it's my husband who has been there for me in my most difficult times. Like my first cancer scare when all my girlfriends ran for cover. He was Old Faithful, remaining by my side through the whole ordeal."

Pauline took a drag on the cigarette, and asked her follow-up with one eyebrow raised. "Does your husband like guys?"

"No, he's just very understanding," the doctor replied, blowing smoke out of the corner of her mouth. "We have an arrangement, a partnership, that works for us. I ask no questions about whom he sleeps with and vice versa. To the outside world, we live perfectly respectable lives but we have our share of fun. Apart and together. My husband doesn't want me to abandon my kind of life, my quest. In fact, he supports me in it, enables me to explore it to the limit. And for that, his openness, his unquestioning support, I'll always love him."

"I don't get it," Pauline said, frowning, one eyebrow raised. "What could you possibly have in common?"

"I feel safe with him," the doctor replied. "He's a great guy."

Pauline smiled charmingly, thinking of diseases, and asked in a meek little voice. "I've always been attracted to you, but I didn't know what to do about it. I've never been involved with intimately with a woman."

"I know you are attracted to me," the doctor said. I could feel it. I feel the same way about you. I didn't want to seem forward or too aggressive.""

Shocked by something mean in the doctor's voice, Pauline nodded weakly, then added a new wrinkle. "I lied. I have two kids, a boy and a girl."

Dr. Gooding didn't look completely happy but she walked over to one of the wall cabinets and removed a stack of blankets and pillows. "Pauline, do you think if we make love—and that's just what it'll be— that'll make you any less of a wife or mother? It really won't. It'll just be our expression of affection for each other. Just between us."

"Brenda, I think I could get attached to you," Pauline said, stifling a nervous gasp. "Sometimes I wish I could be you. You're always so feminine and womanly in the sessions. So soft, confident and sweet."

"Don't worry, honey, trust me," the doctor said, moving up on the young woman, into her until her knee pressed suggestively into the front of Pauline's dress against her sex. The pressure on the hot spot made her client moan and weaken, the space between the women disappeared to a breath, and the doctor's comforting words bombarded her resistance. Her heart pulsed in her throat and stopped when the doctor's tongue traveled that treasured distance from the back of her ear to the small hollow between her neck and chest. The doctor sighed and unbuttoned Pauline's blouse, cooing to her the whole time, looking at her beauty and longing to taste her. To screw her. fter the blouse, next came the skirt, slid around to the side and unfastened, and dropped in a pool on the pine floor. And the bright red panties, wet in the crotch. The doctor kissed her long and passionately, teasing the corners of her lover's lips with the tip of her tongue while she pinched and teased her nipples with her fingers until they felt like tiny stones. Occasionally, the doctor halted her seduction just to look at the disturbingly beautiful specimen of womanhood in her arms, wanting her increasingly more with each new glance. Easing her down on the soft pallet of blankets and pillows, with a stick of Champa incense burning behind them, her mouth alternated between breasts, toying with them until the response of her lover's body told her that she was aflame. The doctor was skilled in this art, so many of her clients had been here, her personal harem. Each woman possessed

146

a weakness, that soft spot, that would melt and yield, no matter how many ways if touched right, if touched with the right tenderness, if touched at the right time. As the doctor rubbed the front of Pauline's pussy, feeling the beginning of the woman's surrender, she kissed her from head to toe, pausing to run one hand soft as an echo along her thighs to feed her need, her urgency. It felt so good to Pauline that she chanted in her head that it was just sex, that she wasn't gay, that it was just need. Or something. She heard the doctor say she wanted to taste her, to eat her. On all fours, the doctor lowered her face to the sweet brown opening and spread her thighs with her hands to expose the folds of her lover's red cherry. She worked her tongue inside, then around the lips, circling the hard pearl in three lazy rotations before going back into her depths. Far off, she heard Pauline breathing hard and moaning, "Yes, baby…oh, yes…oh, please don't stop." The doctor, seeking complete victory over her will, filled that juicy space of desire with her tongue, making her yell out more. She wanted to break her down. The taste of the woman was sweet, almost tart like a ripe lemon.

When the cries subsided, the doctor leaned forward to probe her with her tongue, combining it with her fingers in the gap, slowly to suck her clit and stretch it between her lips, making Pauline's hips tremble and legs shake. She kept on at her with her mouth, prompting her client to grind into her face to seize as much of that magic tongue as she could. Finally, Pauline was yanking the doctor by the hair, her head slumped forward, and pumping away, but the doctor changed up, flipped her, parting her butt cheeks to hit her slit with a series of licks from behind. Pauline, in complete lust, lifted up and lowered herself on the tongue, clamping it with her lower muscles, and then the honey came in a torrent, and her body jerked and shook. The doctor's fingers worked the inside walls of the young woman's opening, making her scream for the doctor to not steal her mind as well as her heart.

Compassionate, the doctor hugged Pauline while she reached the second orgasm, holding her until her breathing returned to almost normal. She rubbed her shoulder, kissed her sweat-tangled hair, telling her to close her eyes. To relax her for the next stage of the seduction, the doctor positioned her pelvis against the younger woman in a vee, their mounds touching, and they began rubbing their clits together. Both shivered with pleasure from the sensation of the ultra-sensitive flesh kissing boldly, the nerves tingling and alive with heat. She touched Pauline's clit lightly with a vibrator, held it fast for a couple of minutes, but put it away.

"I want you so badly" the doctor murmured hoarsely, standing to seek out an exquisite black enamel Chinese box. "Keep your eyes closed, darling."

Pauline was totally her slave, totally receptive. After tracing her finger with gel around her client's red, pouting sex, the doctor got on her knees, lapped at her clit once or twice, and smeared more lubricant on the large flesh-toned dildo strapped to her pelvis. Made of a soft plastic, her husband had recommended the toy to her with the highest praise. It felt like real skin, he said. She christened it "Buster." She held Pauline's legs back, almost over her head to make her fully open for the ten-inch man-made weapon, then dropped carefully toward her target. Pauline flinched, gasped as it went beyond the tip, then began moving in a rolling motion against the doctor's dick. Soon she was taking in more of its length, almost all of it, and clutching the doctor against her, the toy deep and solid inside her. The woman held her own ankles, telling the doctor to grab her rear and ram her against the stiff, well-lubed dildo. They thrusted harder into each other and she was taking it even farther, with the doctor panting and slapping herself into her client with total abandon, rubbing her own clit in the process. She could tell Pauline was cumming again, cumming again hard, her nails clawing at the doctor's soft shoulders, drawing blood this time. They got off at the same time, both moaning and shouting in harmony. Nodding in silent agreement, they tried for one more orgasm before their stamina failed them, and they fell asleep in each other's arms.

Dr. Gooding's husband, a balding man with a mustard complexion and a swimmer's body, woke her up, smiling like a lottery winner. "What a show! You two were fabulous together. She's one of the best ones yet. Loved that little thing you did with Buster. Sure did wear your ass out, girl."

"Are you satisfied, dear?" his wife asked. "Did I please you?"

"Yes, as always," he replied, kissing her on the cheek. "Why the sullen look?"

148

"Goodie, I think I feel something for this girl," his wife said. "I don't know what it is, but it was different this time. I really like this girl. I don't like this game anymore. We're toying with these women's hearts and minds. I want out."

"What are you saying, dear?" Her husband wore a weary face.

The doctor struggled to her feet, hugged her man and looked down at the sleeping woman. "God, I need a cigarette. Did you get it all on tape, babe? She was the best by far. Did you know she had kids, two of them? Sweetheart, do me a favor?"

"Sure. What do you want done?"

"Destroy this tape, Goodie," his wife insisted. "We need to talk later about what we're doing with our little sexual games. I mean, really talk. I'm tired of it all."

Her husband, Mervyn, handed his wife a cigarette and bent down to examine the features of the woman closer. A tasty bit of trade, eh?" he remarked, glancing at her glistening behind. "Why don't we get her cleaned up and back home? You can tell the husband something, one of your little white lies to appease him. Then we'll let you take a nap for an hour or so before we go to Edgar's soiree out on the island tonight. Stan and Linda are driving out with us. One of his sons has his car on a date. Stan said to remind you to bring toys, two bottles of merlot and a corkscrew. He said to get ready to party all night."

He could hear her talking to her new lover in whispers, soft, tender words, and for the first time in their long marriage, a pang of jealousy struck him. In two minutes, he would repeat what Stan had said on the phone and maybe she would be listening this time.

A QUESTION OF DESIRE

The flight from Los Angeles to Rio was exhausting after a week of hasty preparation, quarrels with the family, debates with employers over time owed, and withdrawals of funds from various banks. They were barely recovered from the rigors of a wedding, and the bad hotel service at the secluded inn in Malibu. While Devon, the bride, complained of jet lag and a hangover, she was first to compliment the Brazilian music on the plane, a healthy dose of Jobim, Gal Costa, Astrud Gilberto, Luiz Bonfa and Laurindo Almeida. Twice the stewardess warned her to restrain herself from dancing in the aisles, intoxicated with the bouncy, lilting beat. Harry, the groom, listened to his new wife tirelessly explain their hectic schedule for seeing the sights as the plane touched down in Brazil.

Once they arrived at the Copacabana Palace Hotel, the oldest and most revered accommodations in the city, Devon started her routine again, her renowned flirting that made every hot-blooded male in her vicinity want her. While the hotel manager, a Brazilian man with a strong, hard body, gave them the customary lecture on the former tenants of the plush, expensively furnished suites, his eyes were completely locked on her extraordinarily beautiful frame and little else. He rattled off the names of the hotel's illustrious customers: Josephine Baker, Orson Welles, Jayne Mansfield, in a voice that seemed distant. She did her usual number, tossing her long black mane of hair, giggling, sway-ing her hips, licking her lips repeatedly and pushing out her chest. Her husband was used to this act. She was unquestionably black and stun-ning. And she knew it.

Winking seductively at the manager, she sighed and asked in a low, throaty tone, "Could you be a sweetheart and send me up a large fruit salad? I'm so hungry. If I don't get something into my mouth quick, I might just start eating someone around here."

The manager blushed and glanced at her husband, who grabbed her by the arm and led her toward the bank of elevators along the far wall. Her walk, full of wiggle and heated suggestion, was a miracle of under-stated lust and fire. At the elevators, she paused once more to give the crowd of men gathering at the front desk another taunting look at what could never be theirs. Every man there imagined what it would be like to wear her husband's shoes for just one blessed evening. Just one hour.

Upstairs, Devon paced the suite restlessly, going from one window to the next. "Come on, honey, let's go out," she begged, glancing through the panels of glass at the fabled Sugarloaf Mountain and the glittering blue water of Guanabara Bay in the distance.

Her husband took off his clothes, hung them up, and plopped on the bed in his underwear. "Baby, I'm wiped out. I can't move. The flight zapped me. Maybe we can go out later to see the Carnival fun and stuff. How about that?"

"What are you going to do now?"

He shifted and turned on the bed. "Get some rest. My head feels like there's a hot knife scraping around in it. Can you look in the bath-room and see if there's some aspirin in there?"

"This is unfair, Harry," she shouted, stomping her foot. "Not fair at all."

"What is not fair, honey?" He still was turned away from her on the bed.

Boy, was she pissed off! This honeymoon to Rio was something she had been eagerly anticipating for as long as she could remember. Before they even planned the catering for the wedding reception, she'd rushed out to buy a slew of books on Rio and Brazil, and studied them to get a good idea of how to fill the days of their honeymoon. It was a shame

Cole Riley

that Harry was acting like this, ruining everything.

With a sneer on her face, she watched him sleeping. Then she walked over to the mirror and looked at herself. Damn! She refused to spend her days and nights locked away in a hotel room when the entire city was roaring with activity during Carnival. She sat on the bed in her panties and bra, weighing her options for the night. After a shower, she dressed in one of her most provocative outfits, a short black number with a long slit up the side revealing a full glimpse of leg and thigh. Heads turned once more when she walked slowly through the hotel lobby and out into the madness of nighttime Rio and its frantic celebration of sin and flesh.

It was as if all of the city's eight million people were in the streets dancing, singing and shouting. In the casual manner of the American woman, she walked among the throng, occasionally getting carried away by the Afro-Brazilian beat of the drummers to do a few steps with whatever man happened to be nearby. Her meandering took her along the rows of boarded-up banks and other businesses along Avenida Rio Blanco where the first of the parades was just getting underway. As she was pressed in the rush of the pushing mass of bodies, she flashed on the warning given her by the hotel manager to watch out for pickpockets, but she didn't have her purse with her so there was no reason to worry. Behind a lengthy procession of brightly costumed dancers and drummers came an elegant, fully adorned float, upon which sat a regally gowned young woman, a true beauty waving to her admirers. The Queen. Squads of policemen kept the onlookers a safe distance from the monarch and her sensational float, which was pulled by a small truck. For several minutes, Devon watched the procession before hunger gripped her, sending her in search of one of the restaurants her friend Andrea told her about, with good food and native atmosphere.

On a side street not far from the parade route, she found a place, The Carioca, where she thought the food might be decent. A waiter, speaking in halting English, quickly seated her at the bar until one of the tables became available in the dimly lit room. It took only a few minutes before a man, very bronze and handsome in that typical Brazilian macho way, sat down beside her.

His chair was very close to hers. At first, he didn't appear to notice

152

her but soon she felt a hand under the bar on her leg. The caress was unexpected but very welcome. God, she was so mad at Harry! He'd not touched her once since they said their vows, and that was bothering her. She was horny, simmering with desire, and needed some attention— fast. After a drink, she sat waiting for the stranger to make his move. He didn't disappoint her, for he turned in his seat and asked her in rather polished English if she didn't want to leave and go somewhere where they could be alone. She nodded yes.

They left and walked through the crowd along the avenues to a small hotel where they wasted very little time getting down to business. She didn't feel any real guilt because Harry often told her that theirs would be an open marriage, free of the usual constraints and restrictions of the common union.

It was as if the stranger was reading her mind and knew her situation. There were no attempts at useless conversation. Once in his hotel room, he planted a sultry kiss on her lips, forcing his tongue into her mouth. She turned away, and his huge brown hand covered one of her breasts, pulling at the nipple lightly. What was his game? She hoped he wasn't some kind of fiend or pervert. But then it was a little late for second thoughts. Slowly he lowered her to the carpeted floor, his body pressed snugly against her, and the pipelike length of his erection could be felt through the light fabric of her black dress. He smiled, hiking up her dress, sliding down her panties just enough for his hand to disappear between her legs. Her sex was sopping wet and craving more of the man's attention. When the man touched her, she couldn't stop trembling with excitement and wanting.

"Is this what you want, my beauty?" he asked her in his accented English.

She replied in a whisper. "Yes...it's what I need."

Hot from his constant caresses, she wanted him in her mouth, to taste him, but he had other ideas. He needed to kiss and hold her before he made love to her. Not to be denied, she reached down, grabbed his dick, and brought it to her lips. Surprised, he leaned back on his elbows and watched her lick the engorged head, circle the tip of it with her tongue, flick sweetly and lightly along the tender skin between his balls and anus. There was something about the responses heard in his whimpering and moans that made her even wetter. When she felt him about to explode, she grabbed his dick, squeezed it once to halt the flow of semen, and shoved it back into her mouth. His eyes rolled up in his head. She gagged once as it puffed up inside her mouth, the head ballooning in size, and pulled it out just in time to feel the spray shoot all over her face. She was really wet now, wanting him inside her. The man took his time, putting his face down into her moist cave, sucking and nibbling her nub before he mounted her, entering her doggy-style. His thrusts were rhythmic, slow and steady, like the African beats of an expert samba drummer, and at times his dick seemed to be climbing up her spine. Her legs shook uncontrollably. He held her in place, continuing to ram into her with that steady rhythm until her dam of passion finally crumbled. She wanted to push him away because she felt herself cumming At the same time, she wanted to hold him fast against her body, grip him tighter while he ravished her with his relentless thrusts. The orgasm began in her center, echoed out along her limbs, and finally made a sudden ascent up to the crown of her head. He kept on moving in her, reaching under her to cup her swinging breasts while he mumbled in a constant string of sweet Brazilian phrases. He felt like a steel pole in her. She started pushing her rear hard against him, banging against his every deep-penetrating plunge. She yelped once as he climaxed, hard and pulsing, with her and pulled out.

Her Brazilian lover said he was still hot for her and wanted to put it back into her but she said no. She must get back to the hotel. Harry would awaken and miss her, then she'd have some explaining to do. They showered together. Her lover complimented her on how her skin was absolutely glowing, then she left, running back through the crowds of Carnival revelers to the hotel. Before her departure, she told her mystery lover that she'd never forget him, even if she didn't know his name.

Back at the hotel, Harry was stirring, sipping from a glass of Scotch when she walked into the suite. He didn't notice anything different about her. He made a few business calls before joining her in bed. That night, she made love to him but it was rather clumsy and brief. One, two, three, and he fell asleep. She laid in the bed beside him, remembering her time of passion with the stranger, reliving every kiss, every touch, every thrust.

154

That next morning, she was up early, showered, dressed and ready for the day. Harry moved a little slower, but he seemed somehow energized by the night's sleep. Since he was a gambler by trade, he was inquiring through contacts and croupiers about the game rooms and the action at the tables at the various hotels. He mentioned to her that he wanted to take in a few sessions at the casinos before they went back to the States. Also, there was a black-tie dinner Sunday at one of the larger Zona Sul beach hotels which he wanted them to attend so he could check out a few marks for some quick hustling and easy scores. She said it was no problem for her; she'd be glad to tag along.

While she shaved her legs and complained about having nothing to wear, he casually asked where had she gone the night before.

"I was restless so I went out for a walk," she said, not saying anything about her love session with the stranger.

"Anything interesting happen, baby?" He was trying to fit his loud-colored beach shirt into his tight-fitting jeans.

"No, not really," she replied, watching him apply aftershave to his craggy face.

About a half hour later, the couple was strolling along the famed Ipanema Beach, one of the city's more treasured stretches of sand, watching the scantily clad sun worshippers. Indeed, nothing about Rio could be put into a category, the place, the food, the sights or the people. Both Devon and Harry couldn't take their eyes off the men and women, tributes to God's mastery of construction, each more eye-popping than the last as they strutted along the beach. Harry told her that the women were the most beautiful in the world, without a doubt. Once or twice, he almost snapped his neck trying to catch a look at some devastating lovely female, her wonderfully tan breasts exposed and butt cheeks bare with only a sliver of cloth concealing the mystery of her sex. He took pictures of every tall, luscious woman that caught his eye. They were everywhere he turned, these heart-stopping, delicious specimens of femininity, sex and curves.

When the sun became too hot, they set off for the far end of the beach, stopping to watch the windsurfers riding the waves out on the dark blue water. A boy, no more than ten, walked up and asked to take their picture with Harry's Nikon camera. Harry handed the camera to the boy and stood next to his bride. Before he knew it, the boy backed away, pivoted and started running down the beach. Harry ran after him. Suddenly, a hulking Brazilian man, all muscles and angles, appeared out of nowhere and tackled the young thief, holding him until a winded Harry could arrive.

Harry and the Brazilian were talking with the boy captive between them, when Devon finally reached them. Their hero, standing there like an ad for extreme physical fitness, stared at her openly with critical, appraising blue eyes. Blue eyes in a brown face! His attraction to Devon was not lost on Harry, who was always on the prowl for another new wrinkle in their sexual adventures, and so he invited the man to go with them to a nearby café.

"Let the boy go," the man said after introducing himself as Joao. "He's nothing but a beach rat from one of the nearby *favelas*. They make their living stealing from the tourists who come down to the beaches."

"What is a favela?" Devon asked, smiling at the man.

"It's one of the many shantytowns in the hills above Rio where the poor live," Joao answered. "They are very dangerous, crowded, and even the police stay away from them."

Together, the three new friends crossed the beach after freeing the boy, walking toward the ramp and the street. Joao pointed to one of his favorite cafes a black away from the beach. It was a sidewalk cafe that reminded Devon of the one in Paris along the Seine on the West Bank. The place was crowded. Eventually, they found an empty table and sat down.

"*Boa tarde*," the waiter said warmly. Good afternoon.

The waiter, a light brown man with thick black hair, gave a blinding smile and asked if they wanted to see a menu. Or would they prefer to order drinks?

The trio agreed to start with drinks. As usual, Harry ordered for everyone, gin and tonic. Meanwhile, Joao had not taken his eyes off Devon for one moment. His smile did things to her, sending a feeling like a warm electrical current down her spine to rest between her thighs. The sensation robbed her of her breath and speech for a few seconds but she battled to keep the emotion from registering on her face. He was movie-star handsome. If she took this man back home, the women would be crawling through her apartment windows to get at him.

"Your wife is very beautiful, Harry," Joao said, still looking her directly in the face. "But then you must know this already, yes?"

"You bet I do!" Harry exclaimed, already thinking of how surreal it would be to see this man making love to his wife. It was a sexual fantasy he'd discussed with Devon so many times.

Devon looked away from Joao, felling uncomfortable under his stare. "Are you from Rio, Joao?"

"Yes, I've been here my entire life. Except for a brief time in Bahia."

"Maybe after our drinks, you can accompany us back to our hotel so we can get to know one another a little better," Harry said, hinting of a larger master plan.

"Yes, that would be quite fine," Joao replied, his hand now boldly on Devon's wrist. "Are you enjoying our city so far?"

"Very much," Devon answered, making no attempt to remove his hand from hers.

Joao ordered them a couple of bottles of *chope*, ice-cold Brazilian beer, which they quickly downed after complimenting him on its rich, potent flavor.

They spent another forty minutes at the cafe, talking about the city and Carnival before setting off for the hotel. Strangely, there was some nervous tension among them as they walked along the street as if they knew what was going to happen once they got back to the suite.

At the hotel, Harry fixed more drinks for them, and Devon felt herself relax. By her fourth drink, she found herself staring at Joao's mouth, big and full-lipped, seductive. Harry drank, his nerves as taut as a coiled bedspring, and chattered away about how their sex life was so strong and secure that any experimentation wouldn't threaten either of them. Already he imagined the three of them in bed, exploring one another's bodies.

Devon sat on the sofa between them, curled up with her knees high, and a wide smile on her face. She was down for whatever happened, especially after the other night. Her heart sped up with every glance Joao gave her. A woman and two men. The sexual fantasy of many women, one that they would never admit to a lover or husband. But Harry was different from most men. She knew Harry wanted to watch another man take her sexually while he watched, so she was not surprised when Harry introduced the topic.

"Harry, are you certain you want to go through with this?" she asked.

"Yes, baby. We've talked all about this, and you know how turned it would make me to see you with another man," Harry said, his eyes shining with possibility. "I want you to enjoy yourself."

She sat up, holding Joao by the hand. "But I don't want to change what we have. Men say they want a threesome but afterward they can't get over it. You've got to be sure that you can handle what happens in your head."

"I can." Harry seemed certain. "Baby, I'm ok with this. You forget who you're talking to, you forget the life I've lived."

She suddenly grabbed Joao and pulled him to her, against a wall. He kissed her long and deep, one hand holding her head and the other circling her waist. His hips, actively grinding, pressed into her. He stopped and glanced back and forth between the couple, saw their smiles and started stripping off his pants.

Harry laughed out loud and pumped his fist once in the air before he started removing his clothes as well. When everyone was totally nude, the men knelt before Devon, on hands and knees, as she sat in a chair with her legs parted, revealing her sex. They alternated positions, one kissing and nibbling her nipples into hard rosebuds, while the other lapped at the damp bush between her thighs. Her eyes closed as her pleasure increased, her body swayed with the force of the men's kisses and caresses. After a time, she ordered them to stand before her with their erect dicks near her face, and her mouth went back and forth between them. No words were said after that.

Harry smiled. He never thought his wife would be so gung-ho about this trio idea, but there was much he had to learn about her. She not only played along but seized control of the game. He watched while his wife and the Brazilian moved into the sixty-nine position on the bed, Joao's head between her delectable thighs and Devon's mouth buried in his crotch. She gave Harry one last wink before Joao's tongue brought her to another earth-shattering orgasm, before he lifted her up to straddle him like a cowboy. Her husband pulled up a chair close to the sofa so he could watch her face change in the throes of sexual ecstasy. Joao's mouth pressed hotly on her lips, his powerful arms enclosed her lithe body. She adjusted herself on their new friend, arching her back, feeling him big in her. When the ride got faster and stronger, Joao hoisted her into the air over his stiffness, bench-pressing her bulk with ease up and down on himself until she experienced an orgasm that made her cry out so loudly that the glasses rattled in the room.

"Give it to him, baby," Harry urged, stroking his own rod into a vein-bulging thickness. "Don't hold back. Show me you love me."

The sex fever generated by the hardness of Joao inside her, like soft marble massaging the nerves of her inner walls, erased her fear that her screams and squeals might alarm people on her floor. He held her up with one hand, removed his organ, which was covered with her juices, for her to watch it pulse in his large fingers, before he put it back where it belonged. They moved frantically against each other, their desires building higher, one then another explosion followed. After their bodies jerked and twitched, Harry pulled his wife away from Joao, lifted her face and kissed her. She tried to rear up but finally surrendered upon his entry into her. He was moving in her in ways, new ways, twisting and dipping, inspired by the sight of his wife with another man. For her, he was like a young lover, ardent, passionate and untiring. It got even better when he lifted her legs up on his shoulders, establishing a rhythm she never expected from him.

"Whatever you want, sweetheart," she chanted. "I love you so much."

Without her knowing it at first, she felt two dicks in her at the same time, and the sensation of the double penetration was so overwhelming that she moaned nonstop as both men sought to drive themselves to the limit to satisfy her. The incessant driving pressure of the hardened flesh separated by the thin membrane finally brought an almost unnatural yell tearing from Devon's open throat when a powerful exquisite climax tore through her body.

The men stood afterward and watched her roll away from them, sprawling on the bed. Harry leaned over and stroked her sweat-drenched cheek. She smiled lazily at her husband.

"Baby, I loved it," she murmured, still feeling the ghost of both men still inside her body. "That was different. Yes, that was something else."

Later, after the Brazilian left, they stood at the window watching the procession of samba teams, dancers, costumed revelers and bare-breasted beauties flow past the hotel. Harry bent his elbow, checked his watch. Maybe there was time for one more session. They stayed in the suite all night, pleasing each other, celebrating this new milestone in their young marriage.

THE FLESH IS WEAK

I t is another long weekend after an especially hard work week. Nina calls me at the job, interrupting my stocks meeting with this big tease of a suggestion that we go out to watch some black male erotic dancers at The Warehouse in Harlem. The Warehouse, as it turns out, is just that, a huge warehouse where textiles were processed in the late forties after the war. The place has been closed for years after undergoing several incarnations as a disco hall, carpet-surplus center, health clinic and museum. Now, three enterprising Dominicans own it, running it as an upscale strip club for women, with events every weekend. During the week, it is rented out to various local civic groups.

Nina likes all of this wild stuff, strippers, safe-sex parties, porno, anything having to do with sex. On the other hand, I'm just Lorraine, quiet, simple, hardworking and very moral. I toil as a stockbroker at a Wall Street trading company. You'd know the name if I said it. I've never lost touch with my roots or who I am. Still, Nina is on a mission to yank me into the Twenty-first Century as a modern woman, socially daring, morally challenged, and sexually aggressive. But I'm not an easy case so she devotes much of her spare time to my redemption, rehabilitation and renewal.

You were the first thing I saw when we got to the club. The announcer, another well-built stripper, said your name was Drum.

161

Believe me, it should have been Mandingo, because you were one of the finest specimen of Black Man I've ever seen. I work out on a regular basis, and, honey, you were the bomb. All chocolate, all muscle, all covered in sweat. You have those women, all four hundred of them, screaming and going buck wild up in there. I couldn't figure you out. You were constructed like a devoted bodybuilder, all rock-hard contours, but you move like a headliner with the Alvin Ailey dance troupe. Boy, you took that stage like you owned it. The security guys have trouble restraining these hot and horny women once you really got into your thing, they were bum-rushing the stage, throwing money, throwing panties, throwing themselves. Throwing everything at you. You turn each and every one of these females into hysterical, sopping-wet-between-the-legs superfreaks. I love every minute of it.

Now Nina has a guy pal who got us good seats right up front, so every time you do a new move, a shower of crumpled bills would sail right over our heads. A few fell into our laps but security didn't miss a trick. They swooped down on those bills before I could even see what domination they were. But I'm serious, I've never seen anything like it. You had these sistas fighting one another to get close to the stage, tearing at their clothes, panting and carrying on.

One woman reached over me when you got close to where we were and felt you down there, copped a feel of your oversized bulge tucked into that pouch between your legs. She shouted as loud as she could: "Girlfriend, the dick is mine."

Dancing for a living shouldn't be hazardous work. Irv, one of the guys at the job who goes to titty bars a lot, says men aren't allowed to touch the women strippers at those clubs but here it seemed anything was possible. Here, the level of contact is off the hook. These women were fierce. They were going after anything with a bulge. But you were cool, careful to spread your attention around to all of them, teasing a high-yellow sweetie at the end of the row, then jumping down into the crowd to titillate some plus-size cutie with a nice face. You were democratic in your antics, leaving nobody behind. Everybody got a taste or a sniff or a feel.

So Sisqo's "Thong Song" is jamming behind you and you prance out to this girl, literally pick her up bodily, bring her to the stage, lay her

162

down and wiggle and shake your crotch in her face. And she's loving every second of it. In fact, you have to hold her hands so she doesn't maim your privates, holding them firm at the wrists. Then you kneel over her, pull her dress over you, your head down between her legs as you pretend to taste her. The whole place roars its encouragement. The woman on my left screams for you to take your time and let the girl get hers, and everybody cracks up.

Nina turns and nudges me. She says she comes here a lot on the weekends. The joint is always packed. Standing room only sometimes. She says one woman, a good-looking sista, pushed another sista aside and literally snatched Drum's dick out of its pouch and popped that bad boy right in her mouth. Sucked that thing like a pacifier until she was separated from the meat.

Now you are on stage tormenting another woman, a stout, dark sista, by grinding all against her butt. The music now is by DMX, that hunky rapper with the muscles and bald head. You have hair, lots of it, a mane of long, thick braids. A prowling black lion. You move like an endless wave all along the broadness of the woman, who plays to the crowd by fanning herself. But every woman there knows if someone put their fingers down in her panties, they'd be soaked through. They all laugh but there's not one there who would not switch places with her. The crowd screams again when you lip-synch the words to the R&B anthem for soulful swingers, "The Freaks Come Out at Night," undulating your entire body like a cobra about to strike, curling and snapping your pliable spine like a whip in mid-air, taking a new victim from behind and whirling her to delightful air kisses on her nipples before flipping her into a sixty-nine pose. That makes my nipples hard, and sparks fly deep in my love canal, Mr. Man. I become one of them, one of your fans right then and there.

Suddenly, you're all up in my face, grinning wickedly, and the howling women are still grabbing at you, reaching all over me to get at you, at your marbled chest, at your bubble behind, at that obscenely huge bulge in that pouch. Before I know anything, you've got me flying up through the forest of hands to your big shoulders, dress flying, yanked around with my sex right up against your mouth. You blow it a lewd kiss and then a couple of toots of hot air. I swear you winked at me

Cole Riley

before you hoist me back up above your head like a circus performer and sit me down in my chair. I am totally breathless and more excited than a jailed wife on visiting day.

Nina laughs like a madman. "Girl, did he kiss it?" she asks, grinning from ear to ear. I am speechless, completely flustered, and stay that way for the remainder of his show. The throbbing is so strong that I wonder if my face also betrays my arousal. The entire hall is on its feet cheering and clapping as you make your exit after bowing and wrapping that fine body in a large red beach towel. I turn, and it is then I notice that Nina is gone. I wait for some time before I head toward the backstage area.

"Hey, girl, I have a surprise for you." It is Nina waving frantically at me. You can't take some people anywhere.

And you were on her arm, standing with your large, muscular arms folded across your chest. You flash me a smile as I walk toward the pair of you.

"Your friend here says you'd like a private show," you say.

I glance at Nina in disbelief. "Oh, I didn't say that."

"Well...your friend Nina says she'll pay for all expenses," you say, looking deep into my eyes while folding a slip of paper. "I have your address. Everything's arranged. I'll be there tomorrow night at eight-thirty. Wear something comfortable. It's your night out...or rather in."

In the cab back to my apartment, I sulk at first but I understand what my friend is trying to do. I couldn't remember the last time I had fun, real fun. Since I was the oldest girl in my family, I was responsible for everyone else, from taking care of my aging parents to getting my younger brother out of a legal jam. Ask Nina. But this would be my night, as you said, hot fun delivered right to my doorstep.

The doorman calls up and says I've got a visitor. I tell him to send you up. All day, I worked on the apartment, getting it together. I wear a flowing yellow summer skirt and a simple top. The perfect attire to seduce a man, right? Just shows you how long it's been. No sooner are you in the door than you start dancing in the middle of my living room, giving me a show that makes me want to tackle you right there. On one tune, "Sexual Healing," you stand inches from my face, all of your stuff there within reach, the full outline of it so teasing and tempting. You

164

spread your legs, lift one leg straight up in the air, and I can see how impressive your meat really is.

When you drop to the floor, pumping your pelvis in hammering plunges on the hardwood, I again become no different than the other screaming women at that strip show, yelling as if you were inside me, your firm meat up in there. You flip over and motion for me to join you on the floor, to climb on top of you. Since I'm an average-sized woman, it seems like a sudden shock of the senses when my body covers your chocolate mountain of damp, muscled flesh. That close, my nose picks up the mixed scent of your masculine musk, soap and aftershave. Instantly, you gain control of the situation by sliding under me, gripping the cheeks of my butt, angling me so that I'm now straddling your face. Much like the other night at the show. I gasp, but that doesn't stop you from making a wet outline of my swollen lower lips with well-placed flicks of your tongue. I could tell you were a guy who loved making women happy.

"Do you realize how wet you are, Lorraine?" These were your first words of the night. "Your friend says I'm to give you the Queen treatment, that means you get full-service care and pampering."

"Is this something you usually do in your line of work? Servicing women?"

Your voice is slightly muffled because your face is bracketed by my legs. "No, I'm not a whore if that's what you're saying. This is something I'm doing for the friend of a friend. Besides, I think you're rather beautiful."

"So are you!" The words come from my throat without too much prompting.

"Has anybody ever told you that you look like Nancy Wilson, the jazz singer? My mother's a crazed fan of hers, has everything the woman ever recorded. You look just like her. The young Nancy. Anybody ever tell you that?"

I am flattered but tell the truth. "All the time. My friends say it too."

You get up from the floor and give me your hand. "This is your night. Let's do it right. Ok?"

I nod, start to turn around to go back to the sofa when you take me

Cole Riley

in your arms and give me a long, gentle, sensuous kiss. The kind that takes your breath away and makes your legs weak. You smile once more as you slowly undress me, removing my blouse to cover my dark nipples with your hot mouth, licking and sucking them. As I struggle to catch my breath, you run your tongue along the long contour of my neck, leaving a searing line of flame from its nape to that most sensitive spot right under my ear. So we are both caught up in the whirlwind of desire and lust, kissing and caressing each other to feed the growing need within us. I've waited a long time for a moment like this, too much time has passed since I was loved, and I let you know it by the way I move against you, rapidly losing control and not giving a damn about it. You ease me back on the sofa, skillfully pull down my panties, remove my dress, so you can take me to another peak of wanting. When your mouth trails my inner thigh, I gasp and resist the temptation to lock your head there with my legs.

"Take your time, please," I pant. You smile up at me.

Your fingers delicately part the inflamed lips of my sex, your tongue darts into its secret places, sparing nothing in its sweep. I put one leg over your shoulder so you explore my entrance with your fingers, inserting them, ramming me with them until I feel so close to orgasm that tears well in my eyes. You play with my heat, taking out the fingers and replacing them with your tongue. Shivers rack my body, legs trembling, hips rising off the sofa, and my explosion is not far off. I can hear nothing but the soft sounds of your breathing, the air rushing through my pubic hair from your nose, your tongue worrying my pussy while your thumb massages my aching clit. I am yours. You take my protruding clit and make it your own. My pelvis widens even more, begging for more than your fingers and tongue as my cries become shouts of joy and lust.

"Yes, yes, baby, give it all to me," I whimper, clinging to you tightly to stay above the rising seas of torrid emotion. "Don't make me wait, please."

But you did wait, waited until my entire body began to writhe from the heat, before you stroke my face with a gentle hand and repeat "This is your night." You stop everything, holding me by the shoulders, and stare deeply into my eyes. You have more than technique; this is art of

166

the highest order. You kiss my eyes, forehead, nose, then close with the softest kiss ever on my lips. That one move alone makes my heart rattle within my ribs, but no more than your kisses along the whole length of my body, from head to toe. What a lover! What skill!

You stop the kisses and scoot back from me. "You know, you don't have to go through with this if you don't want to. You call the shots here. All you have to say is stop, and it's over."

I try not to stutter. "I want you. I've wanted you from the moment I saw you on that stage. I wanted you to make love to me just as you are doing right now. Don't kill this night, don't. I must have you…inside me."

Your lips press tenderly into mine. Your strong but caring touch warms me. You go down on me three times more, always stopping at the brink, driving me mad, stoking the fire. It's pure bliss. Whispering that you've been waiting for this, you enter me, responding to my urgent shouts to "fuck your pussy, fuck it baby," going at it like this is our last time. God, it was the best. You hit places in me that I didn't know existed. It is as if you have a detailed map of the walls of my vagina and touched just the right spots to make me totally helpless. I lose count of how many times I came before you clench me tight, roar out your pleasure and fill me with your juice. I can't ever remember cumming so hard, so often.

Afterward, we shower, joke about our workout and share a chilled bottle of Moet, something I had saved in the fridge for just this occasion. We toast our newfound friendship, Nina's timing and the horny gals at The Warehouse. We laugh and talk for hours, almost till morning.

As I kiss you good morning, you kiss my nose and say with an impish smile: "Miss L, this is a good start, but next time we'll do a real date. Like normal people." We laugh at that, you hugs me again, and I swat you on your shapely rear as you walk through the door. One thing is certain: I owe Nina big time.

Indigo After Dark Vol. I

By
Nia Dixon and Angelique

Like a musical director who guides an orchestra to a climactic crescendo, Nia Dixon takes you there musically, poetically, and sexually, with her collection of stories, **Midnight Erotic Fantasies**. Her poignant emphasis on female pleasure is told with such awesome detail you'll feel your temperature rising from the first story to the last. She develops a true mixture of erotic fantasies which will send you running to find pleasure in the arms of the one you love.

In Between the Night by Angelique tells of the erotic adventures of Margaret and her sexual awakening from plain Jane by day to the sensual cat on the prowl, Jade, by night. Margaret is both frightened and intrigued by the dark and dangerous feelings that consume her. It is Anthony, a stranger she meets in the park, who brings out the real woman hidden beneath-and now he too is consumed by her fire.

ISBN 1-58571-050-4 $10.95
Order your Indigo After Dark Vol. I today at your favorite bookstore or online at the Genesis Press website. www.genesispress.com.

INDIGO
Winter, Spring & Summer 2001

January

Ambrosia	T. T. Henderson	$8.95

February

The Reluctant Captive	Joyce Jackson	$8.95
Rendezvous with Fate	Jeanne Sumerix	$8.95
Indigo After Dark Vol. I	Angelique/Nia Dixon	$10.95
In Between the Night	Angelique	
Midnight Erotic Fantasies	Nia Dixon	

March

Eve's Prescription	Edwina Martin-Arnold	$8.95
Intimate Intentions	Angie Daniels	$8.95

April

Sweet Tomorrows	Kimberly White	$8.95
Past Promises	Jahmel West	$8.95
Indigo After Dark Vol. II	Dolores Bundy/Cole Riley	$10.95
The Forbidden Art of Desire	Cole Riley	
Erotic Short Stories	Dolores Bundy	

May

Your Precious Love	Sinclair LeBeau	$8.95
After the Vows	Leslie Esdaile	$10.95
(Summer Anthology)	T. T. Henderson	
	Jacquelin Thomas	

June

Subtle Secrets	Wanda Y. Thomas	$8.95
Indigo After Dark Vol. III	Montana Blue/Coco Morena	$10.95
Impulse	Montana Blue	
Erotic Short Stories	Coco Morena	

OTHER GENESIS TITLES

A Dangerous Love	J.M. Jefferies	$8.95
Again My Love	Kayla Perrin	$10.95
A Lighter Shade of Brown	Vicki Andrews	$8.95
All I Ask	Barbara Keaton	$8.95
A Love to Cherish (Hardcover)	Beverly Clark	$15.95
A Love to Cherish (Paperback)	Beverly Clark	$8.95
And Then Came You	Dorothy Love	$8.95
Best of Friends	Natalie Dunbar	$8.95
Bound by Love	Beverly Clark	$8.95
Breeze	Robin Hampton	$10.95
Cajun Heat	Charlene Berry	$8.95
Carless Whispers	Rochelle Alers	$8.95
Caught in a Trap	Andree Michele	$8.95
Chances	Pamela Leigh Star	$8.95
Cypress Wisperings	Phyllis Hamilton	$8.95
Dark Embrace	Crystal Wilson Harris	$8.95
Dark Storm Rising	Chinelu Moore	$10.95
Everlastin' Love	Gay G. Gunn	$10.95
Forever Love	Wanda Y. Thomas	$8.95
Gentle Yearning	Rochelle Alers	$10.95
Glory of Love	Sinclair LeBeau	$10.95
Indescretions	Donna Hill	$8.95
Interlude	Donna Hill	$8.95
Kiss or Keep	Debra Phillips	$8.95
Love Always	Mildred E. Kelly	$10.95
Love Unveiled	Gloria Green	$10.95
Love's Decption	Charlene Berry	$10.95
Mae's Promise	Melody Walcott	$8.95
Midnight Clear	Leslie Esdaile	
(Anthology)	Gwynne Forster	
	Carmen Green	
	Monica Jackson	$10.95
Midnight Magic	Gwynne Forster	$8.95
Midnight Peril	Vicki Andrews	$10.95
Naked Soul (Hardcover)	Gwynee Forster	$15.95
Naked Soul (Paperback)	Gwynne Forster	$8.95
No Regrets (Hardcover)	Mildred E. Riley	$15.95
No Regrets (Paperback)	Mildred E. Riley	$8.95
Nowhere to Run	Gay G. Gunn	$10.95
Passion	T.T. Henderson	$10.95

Path of Fire	T.T. Henderson	$8.95
Picture Perfect	Reon Carter	$8.95
Pride & Joi (Hardcover)	Gay G. Gunn	$15.95
Pride & Joi (Paperback)	Gay G. Gunn	$8.95
Quiet Storm	Donna Hill	$10.95
Reckless Surrender	Rochelle Alers	*$8.95*
Rooms of the Heart	Donna Hill	$8.95
Shades of Desire	Monica White	$8.95
Sin	Crystal Rhodes	$8.95
So Amazing	Sinclair LeBeau	$8.95
Somebody's Someone	Sinclair LeBeau	$8.95
Soul to Soul	Donna Hill	$8.95
The Price of Love	Beverly Clark	$8.95
The Missing Link	Charlyne Dickerson	$8.95
Truly Inseparable (Hardcover)	Wanda Y. Thomas	$15.95
Truly Inseparable (Paperback)	Wanda Y. Thomas	$8.95
Unconditional Love	Alicia Wiggins	$8.95
Whispers in the Night	Dorothy Love	$8.95
Whispers in the Sand	LaFlorya Gauthier	$10.95
Yesterday is Gone	Beverly Clark	*$10.95*

All books are sold in paperback form, unless otherwise noted.
You may order on-line at www.genesis-press.com, by phone at 1-888-463-4461, or mail the order-form in the back of this book.

Shipping Charges:

$4.00 for 1 or 2 books
$5.00 for 3 or 4 books, etc.

Mississippi residents add 7% sales tax.